JENNIFER S. ALDERSON

Death by Gondola

A Springtime Murder in Venice

First published by Traveling Life Press 2022

First edition

ISBN: 9798444524107

This book was professionally typeset on Reedsy.
Find out more at reedsy.com

To my husband, Philip, for introducing me to Venice.

Contents

1

Smooth Sailing

April 22—Day Four of the Wanderlust Tour in Venice, Italy

"It was here, at Chiesa di Sant'Antonin, that Jacopo sought refuge from his pursuers," the local tour guide said as he sprung up onto a low stone wall and pulled his black velvet cape up in front of his body, as if he was fending off an army.

Lana Hansen, tour guide for Wanderlust Tours, watched her group of eight clients take in the caped storyteller's latest yarn. They had spent the past two hours crisscrossing the city with their guide for the Secrets of Venice Theatrical Walking Tour, and this church was the last stop. The young man was dressed as a *codega*, a medieval servant who—before electric streetlights were the norm—would have lit the way for wealthy citizens, telling anecdotes along the way. Even though it was still daytime, to complete the role, he held a heavy-looking cast-iron lantern in one hand, gesturing with it as he spoke.

His richly colored waistcoat, its bright red color accentuated with gold embroidery, seemed to shine in the hot sun. How he managed to wear a cape, waistcoat, long white pants, and black riding boots without perspiring was a mystery to her. She had spent much of their walking tour discreetly wiping the sweat off her face when she thought her clients weren't looking.

The yarns the guide had shared were fascinating, whether true or not, and the special Carnevale theme made it even more interesting, at least to Lana.

From the reactions of her clients, they were equally captivated with their guide, his stories, and the sights they were seeing.

"After resisting several attempts at capture, he stacked up the pews to make a barricade, but his attackers were far better equipped. They used a cannon to break down one of the walls and then murdered Jacopo with the same weapon."

Their guide opened his arms and fell forward off the stone wall, landing onto his knees with his head bowed. After pretending to be dead for a moment, he looked up at his clients and added, "Historical scholars are in dispute as to whether it took one or two cannon shots to fell Jacopo, but it did take place in 1819, so it is understandable that the details are somewhat sketchy."

Carmen Winters, Lana's most skeptical guest, crossed her arms and leaned back as she examined their guide. "That story does not make sense. Are you certain this event really happened, or is it a local legend? Why was there an elephant in Venice in the first place?"

Their guide threw his hand over his heart. "As God is my witness, this story is true. Jacopo the elephant was brought to Venice for the Carnevale celebrations of 1819, during which the emperor of Austria was a royal guest. When the Venetians honored their foreign visitor with an artillery salute, Jacopo broke loose and wreaked havoc throughout the city before taking refuge in the Church of Saint Antonin."

Their guide pointed again to the rather plain white building behind them, sandwiched in between a row of sparsely decorated homes. The only noticeable difference between it and its neighbors was the tall bell tower jutting out of its roof. Lana's group had to crane their necks to see the top because the small square in front of the church butted up against a waterway and bridge. The tall white tower tilted heavily towards the water's edge, reminding Lana of a recent tour she had led through Pisa, Italy.

"Jacopo perished by cannon shot inside of this church in 1819, and his skeleton was given to Padua University's Natural History Museum. It is still in their collection today."

Carmen's lips were still pursed in disbelief, though her traveling companion's mouth was hanging open, as if she was listening to a delightful fairy tale that she hoped was true. Carmen was on vacation with her bestie, an antiques dealer named Rhonda Davis. Both women were in their early fifties and roughly the same height, although Carmen was lean and Rhonda quite plump. From what Lana had gathered so far, Carmen had retired early, yet still taught self-defense classes to women at her local YMCA—likely accounting for her being in such fantastic shape.

George and Chrissy Fretwell had their arms wrapped around each other's waists as they took in the sights. His short, squat form contrasted sharply with his wife's lengthy legs and tiny waist. While Chrissy was probably a beauty queen in her younger days, George was as cute as an English bulldog. Despite their physical differences, the two couldn't seem to keep their hands off of each other. *It may have something to do with his successful investment firm*, Lana thought, then immediately scolded herself for being so catty.

Whereas George was boisterous and social, Chrissy was far more reserved and shared very little of her personal life or feelings with the rest. George told anyone who would listen about his investment firm, but Chrissy's day-to-day activities were still a mystery. Did she work, or was she a housewife? Lana's natural curiosity kicked into overdrive whenever she was near Chrissy, and she found herself listening in on her conversations in the hopes of learning more about her client.

Chrissy always looked as if she had just left a photo shoot, so she must have spent a lot of time perfecting her hair, makeup, and wardrobe. Although she did seem to prefer to let George do the talking, from their brief conversations, she came across as an intelligent woman—not a dumb trophy wife. *I have four more days to puzzle it out*, Lana thought, looking forward to having a mini-mystery to solve.

Trying to figure out what her clients did for a living was one of the mental games she played when she met a new group. Trips through Wanderlust Tours were quite expensive, meaning many of her clients were dual-career couples who sometimes seemed more married to their jobs than their partners. Oftentimes, they were so proud of what they did, they talked about their work during the entire tour. Some even introduced themselves as their occupations. Others seemed to want to forget about their day jobs and get lost in the experience of travel.

Dave and Kathy Windsor, the other married couple on this trip, were no mystery; they had proudly introduced themselves as the owners of Windsor Custom Watercrafts to Lana—and everyone else they had met on the trip. She'd had to chuckle when Dave had added that they were not related to the House of Windsor, the United Kingdom's royal family.

Windsor Custom Watercraft may not have a royal connection, Lana thought, *but their boats are fit for a king.* She knew from personal experience just how fancy their products were. The owner of Wanderlust Tours, Dotty Thompson, had purchased what she called "a little boat" from them a few years back, and Lana had been lucky enough to go out sailing on it a few times. That lovely "little boat" was five times the size of Lana's houseboat and equipped with every amenity imaginable.

The Windsors were standing close to each other, but not touching. So far, the couple acted more like housemates than lovers, at least when they were with the group. Considering they owned and ran a company together, Lana could imagine it was better that they not be too lovey-dovey in public; otherwise, they ran the risk of making their employees uncomfortable.

The couple had invited the last two members of the tour group, a pair of broadly built brothers named Harry and Joe. Both worked as boat builders for the Windsors' company, and this trip had been a surprise gift to thank them for the long hours they had put in to complete an order.

That must have been a really important contract to warrant such a generous gift, Lana thought. She knew for a fact that this weeklong tour of Venice had cost them thousands.

Standing close to Harry and Joe was Tom, a new guide whom Lana was supposed to be training. Before they had met with their clients for the first time, she had spent an afternoon explaining the Wanderlust philosophy on leading tours, before giving him the space to ask her for clarification when he needed it. This hands-off approach was rather unusual for trainees, yet given Tom's extensive experience as a tour guide in Central and South America, she knew he did not need lessons in leading a group through a foreign land. Tom apparently felt the same way because he had not asked her for clarification on anything, as of yet. In fact, they had said very little to each other during the first three days of the tour. Perhaps her feeling that they were different kinds of people and probably wouldn't become good friends was mutual.

Despite the fact that Lana was not certain whether she liked him as a person, Tom did seem to be an extremely capable guide. Considering Dotty was quite short-handed and needed all of the experienced trip leaders she could find, Lana was sure her boss would be glad to keep him on board.

After answering several more questions, their tour guide bid them *adieu*. Her group gathered onto the small bridge next to the church to take in the sights. Only after they stood side by side against the railing did she realize that this was the first time her group had been able to do so. Everywhere else they had been in Venice so far had been so busy that she'd had trouble keeping her group together. All of the stories about the over-tourism in this island-city seemed to be true, Lana thought, reddening slightly when she realized that she and her group were part of the problem.

She pushed those thoughts aside and leaned over the stone railing, breathing in the lightly salted air as she took in the quietness of the streets and charm of the folksy neighborhood. The homes in this area may not have been as elegant as those on the Grand Canal, but they were just as photogenic. Palazzos painted in shades of salmon and ochre rose up from both sides of the waterway. Plaster flaked off some of the buildings, revealing the layers of colors that had been applied over the centuries. Through the many windows, Lana could see simple kitchens and cozy living rooms. Wash hung off lines attached to the wrought-iron balconies, swaying in the soft breeze like streamers at a party.

After spending the first three days of the tour visiting grand palaces and monumental museums, it was a lovely change of pace to see a less-touristed area of the city. Lana joined her guests in taking pictures of the quiet streets, colorful homes, and stream of boats floating under their bridge. The water was a color unlike any she had ever seen; its soupy green-blue texture reminded her of liquid opals as it sparkled in the warm sun.

Carmen stood next to Lana and snapped a photograph. "It doesn't get old, does it? I've visited Venice a dozen times for my work, but I never tire of it."

"It's my first time, but it certainly won't be my last," Lana replied. Swept up by the magic of the moment, she realized only too late her mistake in telling a guest that she had not yet visited the city she was leading them around.

Carmen's eyebrows shot up. "Really? I figured a tour guide would have to know the city intimately before leading a tour through it." Carmen kept her voice low, as if she was embarrassed for Lana and didn't want the rest to hear.

"We usually do," Lana fibbed, "but something happened and I had to switch with another guide at the last minute." When she began working for Wanderlust Tours, every destination she visited was new, simply because she had never been out of the United States before then. Now that she was approaching a year and a half as a guide, she had been back to the same cities multiple times. But that didn't stop Dotty from scheduling her to lead tours to new destinations, something she was grateful for. Although Lana felt more confident when she returned to a familiar place, she did enjoy the exhilaration of exploring a city for the first time.

She glanced around frantically, searching for a reason to change the subject, when Rhonda burst over.

"Would you look at that? A gondola is coming our way." Rhonda's grin was practically splitting her face in two.

Carmen and Lana followed Rhonda's pointed finger to the end of the small canal they were standing over. A long and skinny black boat—arguably the symbol of Venice—was turning onto the small waterway running under their bridge. A man wearing a black-and-white-striped shirt, black pants, and a red bandana around his neck stood at the back, pushing the gondola forward. Sitting on a plush-covered throne inside the center was a young couple, locked in a kiss.

Lana's thoughts immediately turned to her boyfriend, Alex. What she wouldn't have given for him to be here by her side. Strolling around this romantic city brought him constantly to the forefront of her mind. Unfortunately, he was in Berlin working a conference all week. But after her tour ended, he was going to meet her here for a long weekend. She couldn't wait to walk these streets with Alex on her arm.

After the boat was pointed in the right direction, the gondolier began to sing a song fit for an opera. His baritone voice was a joy to listen to, and his words seemed to echo off of the many homes enclosing the waterway.

"I wonder how much extra that costs," Carmen said.

Rhonda smirked at her friend. "What does it matter? I can't think of anything more romantic." She clasped her hands under her chin. "If my Richard was still alive, he would have certainly paid for it."

From what the pair had told her, both Carmen and Rhonda had recently lost their husbands and had turned to each other for comfort and support.

"My Francis would have said it was a waste of money," Carmen said, before closing her eyes and letting her head sway in time with the rhythm. "Perhaps he was wrong. It is a beautiful melody."

Suddenly a second male voice rose up from behind, singing along with the gondolier in perfect time. Lana turned towards the sound, shocked to see that it was her client Harry performing the duet.

The burly boat builder was standing close to the railing, belting out the melody as if he was standing in the center of a podium. Lana never would have imagined that this giant of a man, with his thick beard and the rough hands of a worker, would be capable of producing such angelic sounds.

The crowd on the bridge grew quiet as they listened to the large man and the gondolier sing the rest of the aria. As the last note hung in the air, their audience on land and water burst into applause, causing both men to bow in gratitude.

"How does Harry know that song?" Lana wondered aloud.

"Italian operas are his favorite," Joe, Harry's older sibling, replied. He was as broad as his brother and a half-foot taller, reminding Lana of Paul Bunyan. "He performs with a few local theater groups on the weekends. If he wasn't such a talented craftsman, I'm certain he would have pursued a career in music."

Harry is truly a man of many talents, Lana thought. "That was beautiful," she gushed along with the rest.

The boat builder shrugged off the compliment. "It would have sounded better if I had warmed up my voice first."

"Where to next, Lana?" George asked. He had his hand around Chrissy's waist and her head rested on his shoulder. Both were wearing so much gold that the sunlight reflected off of their wrists and necks, making eye contact difficult.

Lana used a hand to shield the glare as she smiled at her guests. "Back to Saint Mark's Square. We have a reservation at a wonderful little café along the waterfront."

"That's not saying much; everything is on the water here," Chrissy said as her lips pursed. Even though she had not yet complained about any aspect of the tour, Lana sensed that her client was already tiring of the city. *That might be a problem, considering we have four more days to go*, she thought, resolving to watch Chrissy's behavior more carefully and see whether she needed to find another activity for her guest to do. If anything, Lana might be able to book her into the hotel's spa for the day—if that was even Chrissy's thing.

George laughed, then pulled his wife closer and kissed her on the lips. "True, but it still sounds fabulous. Thanks, Lana."

So far, the guests were getting along exceptionally well. The small size of the group seemed to have helped their comradery. Because one couple had to cancel at the last minute due to the wife breaking her hip, there were only eight of them. Given the relaxed pace of this one-city tour, they had lots of time to get to know each other. Luckily, they had found plenty of common ground in the few days they had spent together.

They had already visited the city's most important museums and churches, which—thanks to Venice's compact size and incredible water taxi network—were within easy walking distance from each other. Lana ran a hand over her reasonably taut stomach, glad that the extra exercise allowed her to enjoy the rich Venetian cuisine without feeling guilty about the calories.

"Is that one of Sail Away's new boats?" Dave called out, as he pointed towards a small ship sailing in the lagoon.

Windsor Custom Watercraft had recently built a fleet of small oceangoing vessels for Sail Away Cruises and were in Venice to meet with Matteo Conti, the company's CEO, so they could decide on a delivery date. Harry and Joe seemed incredibly proud of their innovative designs and spoke of how Matteo's requests pushed their abilities to the limit. The photos of the lavish interiors and extensive amenities made Lana want to immediately book a cruise on one of their luxurious vessels.

"It sure looks like the ship they wanted us to emulate," Joe replied, squinting at the watercraft as it sailed into the sun. "What do you think, Harry? Your eyes are better than mine."

"I have to agree with you, brother, though our design is better," Harry said before turning to Joe and slapping his hand in a high-five.

"What do you think, George?" Dave asked.

"I wouldn't know. I don't concern myself with their fleets, only their finances."

From what Lana had gathered so far, George was a major investor in Sail Away Cruises and was here to sign several contracts, as well as see the sights. Matteo Conti had invited him and the Windsors to a special masquerade ball being held at Sail Away Cruises' headquarters tonight. It was thanks to these three guests that Lana and the rest of the tour group were also invited to attend what promised to be a spectacular party.

"It could be. Matteo did say that he recently expanded two of his local fleets, which is why he needs another cash injection to keep growing. Not that I mind him asking me—I'm happy to give him more of my money. Thanks to Matteo's leadership, Sail Away has made me more per dollar than any other investment in my portfolio. If he were a woman, this lady here would be in trouble." George guffawed and ribbed his wife.

Chrissy slapped his chest and growled, "Watch yourself, big boy."

"I cannot tell you what a relief it has been to talk with you about Sail Away Cruises. Since you made clear that they are financially solid, both Dave and I have been able to relax and enjoy the trip more," Kathy gushed.

"I can imagine," George sympathized. "There must be some sort of misunderstanding about the final payment and delivery date. They are solid, otherwise I would be pulling my money out of the company, not investing more in them. Hopefully you can talk to Matteo about it tonight at the party."

Throughout the tour, George could not stop singing Matteo's praises, which had helped to put the Windsors at ease. Matteo had not responded to several of their recent emails, and they had been worried that Sail Away was on the verge of bankruptcy. Since Venice changed its rules regarding the size of cruise ship that could enter the lagoon, many companies that specialized in Italian cruises had run into trouble or even gone belly up. Lana hoped the boat builders were able to speak to Matteo soon, so that they could forget about work and focus on their vacation.

"Speaking of which—Lana, when are we going to pick out our costumes?" Chrissy asked.

"After lunch. The rental shop is a short walk away from the restaurant."

"Then I better not eat too much, otherwise I won't fit into my dress." Her client laughed, her jangly earrings and long blond hair shaking as she did.

Because tonight's party was a Carnevale-themed masquerade ball, Sail Away Cruises had recommended a costume shop where they could rent the traditional gowns and waistcoats that were required dress this evening. According to the shop's website, each costume came with a matching mask, as well. Lana couldn't wait to see which gown she would get to wear, though she was slightly concerned that she was not skinny enough to make the small-waisted designs look good.

"Why don't we head over to the café now? With a little luck, we'll have time to fully digest our meal before we have to try on any clothes," Lana said, waving at her group to follow her down the street on their right. She opened her phone's map, glad she had already preprogrammed their day's destinations in it. The city was tiny, but the maze of streets and bridges often crossed at illogical places, and it was easy to get lost.

They were soon walking through a series of narrow streets that had seen better days. Most of the bar-covered windows bore signs for seedy-looking hotels and shady tourist shops. A few streets further and they were back in a more expensive-looking neighborhood with stores selling designer-brand clothes and handbags. One more turn to the right and they found themselves standing on a bridge that perfectly framed the Ponte dei Sospiri, better known as the Bridge of Sighs.

They had caught glimpses of it earlier in the tour, but were too rushed to stop and get a good look at it. The white limestone bridge, spanning the narrow canal between the Doge's Palace and the prisons, seemed to shimmer as light and shadow danced on its surface.

"They say it's called the Bridge of Sighs because prisoners being returned to their cells would sigh as they caught their final view of Venice through the bridge's bars," Rhonda said.

"That's beautiful," Carmen whispered, her eyes locked on the magnificent structure.

That wouldn't be the adjective I would choose to describe Rhonda's story, Lana thought, shivering as she thought of those poor people locked away in the bowels of the city's jail. When her group grew quiet again, she added, "Legend has it that if a couple kisses in a gondola under the Bridge of Sighs at sunset while the church bells toll, they'll be in love forever."

"We should do that!" Chrissy squealed. "Why don't we rent a gondola tonight and give it a shot?"

"That's a great idea!" George pulled her in close.

Chrissy bit her lip as she studied the bridge. "I bet it'll be busy under there. We might have to try again tomorrow, just to be sure."

"Good thing it's a big bridge. There's room for several gondolas, I suspect," George laughed. "Lana, what time do the church bells toll? And where can we rent a gondola?"

Tom whipped his head around to stare at George as if he was insane for asking. Before he could say anything, Lana said, "Let me find out. I'll search online for you, once we are at the restaurant."

Tom began shaking his head violently as his eyebrows furrowed. Lana dropped back and let her clients walk in front so that she could speak to her fellow guide. "This is part of being a Wanderlust guide. These guests pay thousands to be pampered—don't forget that."

"Reserving an excursion is one thing, but why can't he Google the answer himself?" Tom whispered back.

"These aren't backpackers, Tom. George probably has his assistant do everything for him when he's home. I bet it's second nature for him to delegate." From what Tom had told her about his former employer, the tours were geared towards low-budget travelers who didn't want to deal with the hassle of arranging local transportation, but didn't want to be part of a tour group, either. Tom's job was getting his clients from one city to the next, and nothing more.

"They don't pay us to be their servants, either," Tom hissed in reply.

Before they could continue, Kathy stopped and pointed at a pink sign hanging in an expensive-looking hotel's window. "There's a Mia Bella Day Spa and Salon in Seattle, too. Let me tell you, ladies, I would avoid it like the plague. The hairdresser was more interested in her phone than my hair, and I came out looking like a French poodle. It was the worst perm and coloring I've ever had," Kathy said before gazing up at the sign again. "I wonder if it's the same owner."

"No, it's not," Chrissy snapped. Lana's head jerked towards her, surprised by her guest's sudden reaction.

"Which one of my locations was it? I'll be sure to pay them a visit."

Kathy's face flushed fire-engine red. "Your locations—as in, your salons? Are you the owner? But the name is Italian," she stammered.

George squeezed his wife's shoulder. "You bet she's the owner. Chrissy is brains and beauty in one."

Chrissy nodded at Kathy in acknowledgement, but her expression remained strained. "My father is Italian, and he used to call me *mia bella* when I was little. It's a term of endearment. Let me know which of my locations you visited and I'll make certain you get a refund and a credit for a free treatment."

"The young lady who permed my hair had just gone through a breakup. Maybe she was having a bad day," Kathy stammered, as if she was to blame for the bad perm.

Chrissy rolled her eyes. "Oh, you must mean Samantha. I'm afraid every day was a bad day for her. She didn't last a week, which means you had incredibly bad luck if you got her as stylist. Most of my staff have been with me for years. I do apologize. I want women to come out of my salons feeling prettier and more confident than before they went in, not embarrassed to show their faces."

"That's incredibly kind of you," Kathy whispered, avoiding the other woman's gaze.

"It's the least I can do." Chrissy squeezed her hand, then hooked her arm through her husband's, propelling them forward again.

The group followed along, but came to an abrupt halt a few hundred feet further.

Chrissy had stopped in front of a display of glass vases and was blocking their path. "I have enjoyed the tour so far, but I cannot wait to visit Murano tomorrow," she said, without taking her eyes off of the delicate creations. "It's so tempting to buy up the shop, but I would rather purchase a few larger pieces directly from the glass factories. George brought me back a gorgeous vase last year; it's as if they captured cloud formations inside of the glass. It's mesmerizing. I can't wait to see how they make them."

Rhonda nodded along. "Me, either. I am so glad Wanderlust booked us in on one of those behind-the-scenes factory tours."

"I do think it will be tomorrow's highlight, though the island itself is quite lovely," Lana added, hoping Carmen wouldn't expose her lie. Luckily, her guest kept quiet.

As they came closer to Saint Mark's Square, the number of tourists increased dramatically. *The hotel's receptionist was right*, Lana thought, recalling how the Italian woman had explained that they should avoid the green line, if they wanted to experience the true Venice.

Lana hadn't understood what the receptionist meant, until the young woman pointed it out on a tourist map. A thick green line marked the city's main routes to the major tourist destinations, so that day trippers could see the highlights in a few hours' time.

The receptionist was absolutely correct so far—walking one block to the right or left of that green line often made the difference between having the street to themselves or being squished in like sardines.

The path they were following was on the clearly marked path, she suspected, because the number of people filling the streets seemed to multiply with every block they walked. Luckily, they were currently moving in the same direction as the majority of tourists filling the narrow streets and bridges. Lana wouldn't want to try to fight her way upstream.

"Are we almost there? I need to use the facilities," Kathy said in a quiet voice, directed at Lana.

"We must be getting close to Saint Mark's Square, I can barely move my arms," George joked. When he noticed his wife had stopped in front of another shop, this one selling antique jewelry, he turned back towards her.

"Do you see anything you like, gorgeous?" George asked as he used his hefty frame to push his way around several tourists.

"Sorry, guys, but do you mind waiting to shop until after lunch?" Lana called out. "It's taking longer than I thought to get us to the café because the streets are even busier than I expected. I would hate for us to miss our reservation; the seafood is supposed to be scrumptious."

"Sure, okay, if we can come back after the gown fitting," Chrissy called out, her eyes still focused on a gold necklace with several purple jewels hanging off it, like grapes off a vine.

"No problem, we have a two-hour break afterwards," Lana said, hoping her guest would get moving again. She was having trouble staying rooted to one spot; the forward momentum of the crowd was hard to withstand.

George wrapped his arm around his wife and gently pulled her forward to the rest. "Whatever you want, it's yours."

"Oh, George, you do spoil me." Chrissy kissed her husband on the lips before a woman waving an orange pendant and barking into a microphone pushed them roughly aside. On her heels was a large group of tourists wearing matching blue parkas with a cruise ship's logo on it.

After they had passed, George said, "I'm glad we are a small group. I would hate to have to wear one of those headphones the whole day long."

"That's funny, you don't seem to have any trouble walking around with your telephone stuck to your ear all day," Chrissy said in a teasing voice.

George laughed. "I suppose you're right. But not today." He pointed to his ears, free from electronic devices. "We're on vacation."

"Good boy," his wife replied. "I like having you to myself."

When the two began to kiss again, Lana worked her way to the front of the group, glad to let Tom head up the rear. The couple's public displays of affection only reminded her of how much she missed her boyfriend.

On her heels were Carmen and Rhonda, followed by the Windsor crew. Trailing behind were George, Chrissy, and Tom.

"George sure does love his wife," Carmen said to Rhonda in a loud whisper. "That necklace she was drooling over costs ten thousand dollars! I bet he messed around on her and now she's making him pay for it."

"Oh, you are heartless, Carmen! If anything, he might be worried about her straying. He's not exactly attractive, and Chrissy is worth a fortune," Rhonda murmured back. "I wanted to book a facial with Mia Bella once, but it was so expensive I couldn't bring myself to do it. Considering she's got at least five salons in the greater Seattle area, I bet she's making a killing."

Before Rhonda could continue, Tom yelled out, "Lana, could you wait for us at the next corner? The crowds are making it impossible to keep up!"

She turned around and saw that George, Chrissy, and Tom weren't having much luck getting around the larger groups that kept trundling by. Lana knew that many tourists visited Venice for the day, often as part of a cruise, and only had a few hours to see all of the city's highlights. *If I was in their shoes, I would be rushing around, too*, Lana thought as she backed up against a wall to let another group pass. As she watched another cruise ship's tour guide at work, Lana was thankful that she was not required to wear a fluorescent jacket covered in her employer's name, when she was on duty.

Once her little group was complete again, Lana pressed on, leading them towards the square. Suddenly, the narrow passage they were following opened up, and they were standing on Piazza San Marco. Standing majestically before them was Saint Mark's Tower and on their right was Saint Mark's Basilica, its golden-tiled mosaics and many spires glistening in the sun. The boxlike building behind it was the Palazzo Ducale, or the Doge's Palace. To Lana, the once-royal residence looked like a massive cube resting upon a forest of slender marble columns and arching windows.

During the first three days of the tour, they had crossed Saint Mark's Square several times, yet to Lana, the awe it inspired did not diminish. There were so many beautiful things to absorb, one couldn't take in everything in one go.

She paused to take in the basilica's extravagant exterior. The cathedral was an ornate mishmash of elegant spires, marble pillars, rounded arches, and bulbous domes topped with crosses and pinnacles. A dazzling array of sculptures and mosaics covered much of the facade.

Lana had thought it was odd that this exquisite church seemed to be squished into the corner of this vast square and butted up against the rather somber Doge's Palace, until she learned during yesterday's guided tour that it had originally been built as the palace's chapel.

The cathedral's colorful exterior also contrasted nicely with Saint Mark's Tower opposite. The tall and stately red-brick structure was topped with a white marble bell tower and pyramidal spire, upon which sat a golden weather vane in the form of the archangel Gabriel. The tower, Lana had learned, was originally used as a lighthouse for sailors.

Rhonda had stopped close to Lana and was staring up at the church, her eyes wide as a smile tugged on her lips. "It was such a joy to visit the basilica yesterday. The marble floor, that golden choir screen, and the Byzantine mosaics are breathtaking."

When Rhonda's traveling companion did not respond, Lana thought she would give her client a chance to shine. "What did you think of the interior and mosaics, Carmen?"

"It was incredible to see it all in person," was her concise response. Lana waited for Carmen to elaborate, but apparently her client had nothing more to add.

Carmen was a retired art historian, yet was proving to be quite bashful about sharing her knowledge, to Lana's surprise. Previous art lovers on her tours were constantly relaying anecdotes about the artwork the group was viewing, whether their fellow tourists wanted to hear them or not.

"The cathedral really is a work of art, all on its own. We could have spent days in there and not seen it all," Lana added, getting a smile out of Rhonda.

"Part of me wants to go back during one of our free afternoons, but there are so many other places I want to visit before we leave." Rhonda turned to her traveling companion and smiled. "I guess we'll have to come back to

16

Venice."

"I'm all for it," Carmen replied, "But why don't we see how many of our 'must-see's' we can check off during this trip? That way we won't feel pressured to return right away. There are so many wonderful places to visit in Europe."

"Deal," Rhonda replied.

As they moved further into the massive square, the imposing buildings lining the right side of the public space came into view. Their severe facades were softened by the series of repeating arches lining the arcades on the lower floors. The expansive space in between the monumental buildings was packed full of tourists snapping photos of everything in sight. Large, medieval-looking streetlights dotted the square. Protruding from the top of the tall cast-iron lamps were four arms, each topped with a large glass-enclosed lantern.

Waddling and flying in between them were an absurd number of pigeons and seagulls, hoping for a tasty treat. The city's ban on selling bird seed—as well as the hefty fine for feeding them—apparently hadn't been effective.

When the lagoon came into view, the sight took Lana's breath away. Standing guard were the twin columns of San Marco and San Teodoro, marking what was once the gateway to Venice when the city was only reachable by sea. Resting atop the two marble and granite pillars were the city's patrons. On one stood the winged lion, symbolizing Saint Mark the Evangelist. On the other was a representation of Saint Theodore, the city's first protector, depicted in the act of killing a dragon. To Lana, the mythical beast looked more like a crocodile, but she was still impressed, nonetheless.

Behind them, San Giorgio Maggiore Island and the church bearing its name seemed to shimmer in the hazy midday sun. Lana paused to take in the glorious sight when her fellow guide sidled up alongside of her.

"We are headed to Danieli's Seafood Bar, correct?" he said softly.

"Indeed. The restaurant is just in front of the Doge's Palace—that's the boxy building on our left. Do you want to lead the way?"

His face lit up as his expression softened. "I would. Thanks, Lana."

He winked at her, then turned to their group. "This way, gang," he said confidently before striding off towards the waterfront.

I have to let him take the lead more often and assign him more tasks, Lana reminded herself. It was clear from his reaction that he wanted to do so. And their boss did expect him to be ready to lead a tour by the time their Venice trip was over. Despite his initial resistance to coddling the guests, Lana could not deny that he was qualified to do the job. Once he got the hang of the Wanderlust system, Lana was certain he was going to be a great guide.

Their group followed Tom as he snaked his way through the thick crowds. Lana had just caught sight of the restaurant, when they passed a young child who was tearing up her croissant and throwing pieces at the nearest pigeon.

Uh, oh, Lana muttered. Sure enough, a flock descended rapidly, sending the poor girl into a screaming fit. The birds couldn't be bothered by the girl's cries and kept pecking around her feet, looking for more food.

When the child's father shooed several of them away, they did fly off, but several relieved themselves on the unsuspecting tourists below.

Seconds later, Chrissy let out a shriek that stopped the group in their tracks.

"One of those flying rats got me!" Her arms flailed as she pointed to the blob of bird doo on her shoulder.

George broke into a belly laugh and pulled out a handkerchief. "Did you know that getting pooped on by a bird in Italy is a sign of good luck?"

When she noticed a second dropping on her designer handbag, Chrissy glared up at the culprits and shook her fist at the birds. "I guess I'm the luckiest girl on the planet. At least none of it landed in my hair. I've got so much product in it, the poop might never have come out!"

"I don't know, it would have been an interesting experiment. Guano might be a great new hair treatment," George teased as he helped his wife get cleaned up.

Chrissy's stern expression softened as she began to laugh.

Lana chuckled along with the rest, relieved that her guest could see the humor in the situation. She offered Chrissy a pack of Kleenex, adding, "We are almost at the restaurant. You can clean up properly in their bathroom."

"Good," Chrissy said while dabbing at the large white splotch on her blouse.

Moments later, Danieli's Seafood Bar came into view. Smiles split her guests' faces as they took in the lush tablecloths, crystal glasses, and porcelain plates.

"Classy joint, Lana, well done," George said.

"The thanks go to Dotty Thompson, the owner of Wanderlust Tours. She really knows how to pick a restaurant."

Their tuxedoed waiter showed them to their tables perched along the water's edge before bringing them carafes of sparkling water. As Lana took in the boats bouncing softly on the waves in the lagoon, the churning sea, and the islands in the distance, she could feel the tensions from the past few months melting away.

This may have been the most relaxed tour group she had ever had. Lana prayed that everything would remain as it was for the rest of the week. She just didn't know if she could deal with another murderer on her tour.

2

Lunch on the Water

Their lunch was as exquisite as the view. When they were served their starter—*spaghetti al nero di seppia*—Lana could tell from her guests' reactions that the almost-black dish was not what they had expected. However, once they had sampled the Venetian specialty of pasta prepared with fresh squid ink, the murmurs of approval resounded around the table. Lana joined in, delighted by the dish's earthy flavor and strong fishy taste.

The platters of *fritto misto*, a mix of fried seafood and vegetables, were gone in minutes. The light coating of bread crumbs and squeeze of lemon made each bite a taste sensation. The white wine their waiter insisted they order did complement the seafood-rich meal perfectly.

"Oh, man, I am never going to fit into that dress. Could we take a detour and walk some of this delicious food off?" Chrissy asked after the waiter had cleared their plates.

"Yes, please," Kathy pleaded. "I want to wear one of these sexy dresses tonight, not get stuck wearing a muumuu."

"That sounds like a great idea." Lana was also feeling completely stuffed and dreaded trying on the tight-fitting gowns without having had a chance to digest her meal. She checked her watch and then began mentally planning a longer route to the costume rental shop. "And we have time to do so. The shop is only a short walk away—as is everything in Venice."

After a long walk around San Marco, they doubled back to their destination and arrived in front of the store at their appointed time. A long line of customers trailing out of the costume shop greeted them. Lana wondered just how many people had been invited to the party.

"This is going to take forever," Chrissy whined for the first time. "I hope no one buys that necklace before we get back to the jewelry shop. It was a one-of-a-kind design."

"I'm certain we can talk the jeweler into making you another for you, if someone else does get to it first."

"I suppose," Chrissy said. From her tone, she sounded quite put out. *Is this necklace going to be the breaking point for her?* Lana wondered, hoping the line would move quickly enough that her guests would be able to get back to the jeweler's in time. A whiny guest was a real mood-killer on a tour.

Luckily, the shopkeepers seemed prepared for such large groups because the line of customers moved rapidly in and out of the shop.

Once inside, Lana understood how they could work quickly. One saleslady measured the women's bodices and waists before shouting the measurements to a co-worker, who grabbed a gown and underskirt and shoved them into their client's hands, pointing at a row of fitting rooms at the back of the shop. A salesman measured the width of the men's shoulders and the inside of their legs before grabbing a waistcoat and matching pants for them to try on. The hand gestures and rapid-fire commands indicated that they were to try the dresses and pants on to ensure they fit, and then get out of the shop—pronto.

Lana scurried into one of the fitting rooms and quickly undressed before pulling the underskirt and blue gown on. When she looked into the mirror, she hardly recognized herself. *With the right jewelry, I could be a duchess!* she giggled internally. The dark blue color suited her perfectly, and she loved the way the gold-embroidered accents shimmered slightly in the dim light. The low-cut bustline was going to take some getting used to, but Lana figured as long as she didn't bend over too deeply, it wouldn't be a problem. The dress was tight in the bodice, but not uncomfortably so, and the full underskirt made it seem as if her waist was even smaller than it truly was. Wearing this dress made her feel like a queen.

Knowing they were supposed to hurry up, Lana reluctantly unzipped her gown and pulled it and the underskirt off.

After everyone in her group had tried on their costumes and were satisfied with the way they fit, her guests shuffled towards the exit where another line slowed them down. Two more salespeople were standing in front of a large wall partially filled with traditional Venetian masks, some that would cover the entire face and others only the eyes and nose.

The colorful and flamboyant creations were executed in a wide variety of styles. Some looked like jesters with bells hanging off of their patchwork hats; others were primarily white or gold masks painted with a variety of delicate flowers; and some were completely covered with a rainbow of swirls in a glittery paint that seemed to catch in the light.

Seeing all of these unique creations together like this was beautiful and disturbing at the same time. The masks' haunting eyes and impassive expressions seemed to stare down at her, setting her slightly on edge.

As they passed, a salesperson handed each of them one that complemented the colors of their dress or waistcoat perfectly. Lana was grateful to see that everyone in her group received a half-mask; she could imagine it would feel claustrophobic and rather sweaty to wear a full-face mask all night long.

As soon as they were outside, a bag with a dress or waistcoat in one hand and a mask in the other, the next group was ushered in.

"I can't wait to see what we all look like," Rhonda squealed as she held her bulky bag up.

"Me, either," Chrissy added. "Wearing that dress made me feel like a princess."

"I bet you look ravishing in it," her husband said.

"Just you wait, big boy," she teased.

"Why don't we head back to the hotel and drop these off?" Lana asked, receiving a nod of heads in response.

As they walked back to their hotel, the bags of evening wear swinging on their arms, her female guests began discussing how they should wear their hair tonight and what kind of accessories would be appropriate. Lana was the same—she couldn't wait to try the dress on again and play around with her hair and makeup.

Before they reached the hotel's entrance, George snapped his fingers. "As I recall, I owe you a necklace."

His wide smile stopped Chrissy in her tracks. "That's right, you did promise," she replied before planting a wet kiss on his lips. "That jewelry shop's only a short walk from here. Should we head over now?"

"You lead the way," George said and wrapped his arm around his wife's slender waist.

"Do you need help finding it?" Lana asked, trying in vain to recall exactly where it was. If she remembered correctly, it was in the maze of streets they passed through, right before they reached Saint Mark's Square.

"Nah," George said and smiled at his wife. "Chrissy's got a photographic memory when it comes to things like this."

His wife let out a chortle that stopped them all in their tracks. "You're right about that! When do we need to meet up in the lobby?"

Lana checked her watch. "In two hours. The party's only a short boat ride away. Does that work for you?" she asked, hoping Chrissy wouldn't ask for more time to shop.

"Sure, it won't take long to buy that necklace. That means I'll still have plenty of time to get dressed and properly accessorized. Speaking of which, that necklace should go perfectly with my purple dress." Chrissy grabbed her husband's hand, then waved to the group. "See y'all later!"

A few minutes later, Lana and her group were back in their hotel's lobby.

"Okay gang, we'll see you back down here at five o'clock—in full costume! Don't forget your masks—they are required, as well. They are serving a light dinner and drinks at the party so I would suggest laying off food for a few hours. The menu does look delicious," Lana explained.

When her clients headed up to their rooms, Tom lagged behind. "So what do we do now?"

"The guests have two hours of free time, which means all we have to do is keep our phones on, in case they have questions or problems. But otherwise, we are free to do whatever we want."

Tom's face lit up, until she added, "Oh, I almost forgot, we need to check in with the receptionist and make sure the taxi will be here at five. Would you like to take care of it?"

"Would you mind dealing with the receptionist? I'm not used to holding guests' hands all day long; it'll be good to take a break."

Lana bit her lip, knowing their boss was expecting her to train the new recruits, which also included teaching them how to treat their guests. "I know leading rich people around European cities is a whole lot different than what you used to do in South America. But these aren't backpackers eager to explore the world on their own; they are wealthy business types who pay a whole lot of money to be pampered for a week. I try to think of myself more as their personal assistant than a tour guide. It helps, trust me."

Tom looked at her with narrowing eyes. "What are you trying to say?"

"That holding the clients' hands is part of being a Wanderlust tour guide. I know it can be intense, being with the same group of strangers day and night. I just hope you don't resent having to be on call during the entire tour, that's all."

Tom nodded slowly. "I guess I need a little more time to get used to the Wanderlust way. Knowing that we do have some free time built into the schedule does help. The first three days were so packed full of tours and meals that I figured we wouldn't have any time for ourselves. After all, I took this job so I could see more of Europe."

"Then you chose wisely," Lana affirmed, glad that Tom's attitude wasn't going to be a major problem. "Wanderlust Tours are some of the best on the continent. Now, go enjoy your free time."

"Thanks, Lana." Tom slapped her lightly on the back before heading back out to explore the city.

After she confirmed their taxi with the receptionist, Lana turned to walk away when a young woman tapped on her shoulder.

"Excuse me, I noticed your Wanderlust Tours nametag. Are you leading the tour that Sail Away Cruises paid for?"

I wouldn't quite put it like that, Lana thought, wondering who this young Italian woman might be. It was true that Sail Away Cruises had paid for four of the tickets, but not the rest. "I'm Lana Hansen, the senior guide on this trip. How can I help you?"

The stranger stuck out her hand. "I am Bianca, Matteo Conti's assistant. I have your tickets for tonight's masquerade ball."

Lana eyed the pile of postcard-sized invitations that Bianca pulled out of her bag, smiling in delight. "That's great—how kind of you to hand-deliver them."

The young lady shrugged. "Your hotel is on my way home. Besides, my boss insisted I give them to you personally, instead of leaving them at the desk."

She took a step away from the reception desk and leaned in closer to Lana. "This is the party of the year, and he was worried someone from the hotel might steal your invitations."

Lana's eyebrows shot up. "Oh, that makes the evening sound even more enchanting. Please thank your boss for me."

"You can thank him yourself tonight. I have to go and get ready now. See you later," the young woman said with a wave as she turned towards the door.

Lana's forehead creased as she watched the woman walk away. *What an oddly flippant assistant.* But then, Dotty had told her that Matteo Conti went through personal assistants like Kleenex and that almost every time she sent Sail Away Cruises an email, it was answered by a different person. *He must not be that great of a boss to work for, or the position pays badly*, she figured.

Before Bianca reached the door, Dave and Kathy entered the lobby and also headed towards the exit. "Hey, you're Matteo's assistant, aren't you? I recognize your face from the website," Dave said when he and his wife crossed Bianca's path.

"Yes, I am," she replied in a neutral tone. Yet, when she turned to the couple, her face paled and she began to stammer. "Are you the Windsors? I didn't realize you were in Venice. Didn't Matteo call you?"

Dave and Kathy looked to each other before returning their gaze to Bianca.

"No, he did not," Dave said. "We have been trying to get ahold of him for weeks, but he won't return our calls."

"The last time Matteo made contact was when he invited us to this shindig tonight. That's why we are in Venice. If you are his assistant, why don't you know this?" Kathy asked.

Bianca's face switched from pale to red so quickly that Lana wondered whether the young lady was a chameleon. "There must be a mistake. You would do better to talk to Matteo directly."

She darted towards the door, but Kathy was faster. She stood in front of the younger woman and crossed her arms over her torso. "Not so fast. When is he planning on signing off on the fleet and sending over the final payment? You must know something."

"I really don't," Bianca stuttered. "He never consults me on such matters. I only find out what he's decided when he announces it to the company."

"Listen, lady, we are in Venice for five more days," Dave added. "We have been patient with Matteo so far, but we expect to have this resolved before we leave. Tell your boss we want to set up a face-to-face meeting as soon as possible."

Bianca's eyes were so wide, Lana was momentarily afraid they were going to pop out of her head. When a bellboy dropped a suitcase and its owner began to curse him out, Bianca saw her chance and scurried away from the Windsors and out the door, without answering.

"What kind of assistant is that?" Dave said to his wife as they watched Bianca break into a run.

"I don't know, but her behavior does not make me feel better about this situation. Why is she be surprised to see us here? Matteo invited us over. Heck, Sail Away Cruises paid for this tour!"

"Don't get too discouraged just yet, my pet. We can't forget what George said about their finances. And we haven't worked with Matteo before—you know as well as I do that each client has their own peculiarities."

"Yes, but I didn't expect 'peculiar' to mean being late with payments and not setting a delivery date for a fleet of ships you've ordered," Kathy growled.

"That's true. I know talking shop at a party is usually taboo, but he leaves us little choice," Dave reasoned. "One way or the other, Matteo is going to give us an answer tonight."

3

Calm Before the Storm

"Come on, stay up!" Lana willed her long locks to stay in the hair clip, instead of tumbling out and onto her neck again. Wearing her hair up and hooking the elastic over her bun seemed to be the only way to get her mask to remain firmly on her face, instead of slipping down her nose.

It had taken her much longer than expected to get gussied up in the costume. However, once she took a look at herself in the mirror, she smiled in satisfaction, glad it had been worth the effort.

If only Alex was here to see me in this, she thought as she took a selfie in the mirror to send to her boyfriend later. He would look ravishing in one of the corresponding colorful waistcoats, she suspected.

She checked her watch, glad to see she was only a few minutes late. Fortunately, when she called Tom to ask whether he wouldn't mind keeping an eye on the guests so she didn't have to rush getting dressed, he had been happy to do so. Though Tom was more than capable of the task, she didn't want to leave him hanging too long.

When she emerged from the elevator and crossed to the lobby, the appreciative nods and grins from the male hotel guests she passed made her blush. Lana kept her eyes down as she crossed over to her group.

"You look gorgeous, Lana," Tom said with a leering smile.

"Thanks. I just wish my boyfriend could see me in it," she said, happy to see his smile fade at her words. The last thing she wanted was for a fellow guide to think she was single and interested.

Lana turned to study her clients' colorful costumes. "We all look fabulous." She didn't have to fib. Thanks to their gowns and waistcoats, her clients had been transformed into dukes and duchesses of a bygone era.

"You're right, Lana, everyone looks so distinguished," Rhonda exclaimed.

"I feel like royalty in this gown. I wish I could wear it every day." Chrissy twirled around in her deep purple gown heavily embroidered with gold thread, as her husband nodded in appreciation.

"I won't stop you. You look fantastic," he replied. Lana could hear the lust in his voice. Chrissy's bustline was a little too low for Lana's taste, but George clearly did not mind. He pulled her close and put his mouth to her ear. Whatever he was whispering to his wife was making her giggle. Around Chrissy's neck hung the necklace Carmen claimed cost ten grand.

Lana could hardly keep her eyes off of the gorgeous purple stones or the unique setting. She herself wouldn't dare wear such an expensive piece of jewelry in public, she realized. She would be too concerned about losing it, to truly enjoy the night.

Dave and Kathy looked adorable in their getups, though they were clearly not as relaxed in them as the Fretwells. Harry and Joe looked positively uncomfortable as they tugged on the high collars and hitched up their pants.

"Does everyone have their masks?" Lana asked as she raised hers up in the air. Her guests did the same. When her group began to move towards the exit, she called them back.

"Everyone looks amazing. Before we go, let me take a group picture of you in your costumes. Why don't I take a few without your masks on, first?"

Her group smiled and giggled as they squished closer together for Lana. A small crowd of hotel guests gathered to watch.

This would have been a normal sight two months ago, during Carnevale, but quite unusual in April, Lana realized.

Tom stood by Lana's side and chuckled as he watched the group pose for the camera. After she had taken several, he said softly, "I'll go and see if our cab is here."

"That's wonderful," she replied, grateful that he offered to do it, then raised her voice to get her group's attention. "Okay, gang. Why don't we take some with the masks on?"

Her guests did as asked, transforming themselves into anonymous, expressionless beings again. It was incredible how different they looked, even when only half of their faces was covered. As soon as they were on, the mask changed the person's appearance and immediately added a layer of mystery and anonymity.

A few minutes later, Lana tucked her phone away. "Thanks, everyone. I am certain that I have several good shots. I'll take more pictures at the party and send copies to everyone tomorrow."

"Our chariot awaits," Tom announced when he returned to the group. "Is everyone ready to go?"

"Yes!" was the resounding cry.

Lana practically floated to their cab, excited by the prospects of attending a masquerade ball. She was certain this was going to be a night to remember.

4

Party of the Year

Lana let her masked dance partner swing her to the left, then pull her close and shuffle them forward, keeping in time with the many couples filling the dance floor. Luckily, the stranger appeared to know how to waltz, because Lana was lost. She relaxed her limbs and let her partner lead the way, dreaming that it was Alex behind the face-covering mask and not a complete stranger.

Everywhere she looked, expressionless faces gazed back as they swirled and twirled around the room. There was something surreal about dancing amongst this mass of masked partygoers. In contrast to her group, the majority of guests wore masks that covered their entire face. Elaborate hats and billowy scarves that covered the person's hair and neck completed the ensemble.

Candelabras lit up the rectangular-shaped room, their many candles flickering as the dancers passed by. Silver streamers hanging from the ceiling caught in their light, drawing Lana's attention to the chandeliers the decorations were strung up between. The light fixtures sported several bulbous arms made of glass, blown in a rainbow of pastel colors. Each appendage was topped with a circle of flower-like pedals, from which light emerged. To Lana, each chandelier was a unique piece of artwork.

Waiters dressed in ornately embroidered waistcoats and powdered wigs offered appetizers and glasses of prosecco to the many guests. Lana could imagine that this party was reminiscent of the grander balls taking place during Carnevale, Venice's world-famous pre-Lent celebrations.

The colorful ball gowns and richly embroidered waistcoats that the guests wore were a joy to see. Lana had never worn anything so elegant before and loved the way the wide skirt and frilly underskirt swished against her skin. Nor had she ever attended such a fancy ball before. She felt like Cinderella tonight—all that was missing was her Prince Charming.

When the orchestra's melody faded away, Lana bowed to her partner, wondering whether she should keep dancing or get a drink. Before she could decide, the doors to the balcony opened, and a roar of angry voices infiltrated the ballroom. The orchestra's conductor raised his baton, and the musicians launched into another waltz, drowning out the noise from outside.

A different masked man bowed towards her and offered his hand. She curtseyed back, then off they went, swirling and twirling around the gorgeous space.

As much as she was enjoying herself, Lana couldn't help but think of the voices rising from below, now camouflaged by the music. To enter the party of the year, guests had had to walk through a throng of protesters lining both sides of the red carpet. A wall of security personnel was the only thing keeping the angry mob at bay. Unfortunately, the man of the hour was responsible for their presence.

Lana had learned before this tour that Venice had recently passed a law limiting the size of cruise ships allowed to sail through the lagoon. The city government's decision to finally put this controversial and long-discussed change into law had everything to do with UNESCO's threat to put Venice on its list of endangered cultural heritage sites.

At the same time, Matteo was apparently doing all he could save his business's profit margins. One of Lana's dance partners this evening explained to her that, according to a local paper, Matteo had tried bribing officials to allow Sail Away's smaller cruise ships into the Venice lagoon.

From what Lana understood about the new law, even if Matteo had truly done so, the chance that he would be able to circumvent it was pretty much nil. Too many international organizations were watching to ensure the city government did what was necessary to save its cultural heritage.

Matteo, of course, had denied the accusations vehemently, and he and Sail Away Cruises had even launched a lawsuit accusing the newspaper of slander. Still, it was understandable—and touching—that even a rumor of a deep-pocked company circumventing this long-sought law would mobilize such a large crowd.

Lana pushed the protesters out of her mind as she let herself get lost in the music and dance. Soon, a familiar mask approached. Tom nodded to her as he and his dancing partner passed by. Since they had arrived, Lana had seen him dancing with a different lady for each song. Despite his mask's neutral expression, Lana sensed that he was enjoying himself immensely.

"I don't want this night to end," he laughed as he twirled his current dance partner past her, confirming her suspicion.

"I know what you mean," she replied. It had been months since she had felt so relaxed and happy.

Lana could hardly believe that she was here in Venice, especially after the tragic events that had taken place during her last tour in Seville, Spain. Her boss, Dotty, had wanted to ground Lana after several of her guests had either been killed or arrested for murder during the tours that she and Randy Wright had led together. Yet Lana was certain that she was not a magnet for murderers—that it had simply been bad luck. Now that Randy had retired from guide duty, Lana had convinced Dotty that they had nothing to fear.

So far, so good, she thought. It was day four of the tour, and no one had so much as a splinter. They had visited many beautiful museums, churches, and art galleries, as well as dined at the finest restaurants Venice had to offer. Being here at this party was magical, and definitely the highlight of the trip so far.

As the song ended and her dance partner bowed to her, Lana smiled in delight. This was turning out to be one of the best nights of her life.

5

Temperatures Rising

When a choir of male singers dressed as gondoliers filed into the hall and began to sing, Lana crossed over to the bar to order a Bellini. Although she had never had one before visiting Venice, the bubbly prosecco and peach juice concoction was fast becoming her favorite alcoholic beverage.

As she maneuvered her way through the crowded dance floor and towards the bar, she noticed several men had masks with long, curled noses hanging off of their arms as they swigged their drinks. After dancing for an hour amongst the emotionless masks, it was slightly jarring to see people's facial expressions again.

She sipped her cocktail and glanced over the crowd, attempting to pick out her tour group members mingling among the many.

Thanks to the elaborate costumes and masks the invitees were required to wear, it was almost impossible to tell who was who. Fortunately, Lana had the group photos as reference. She flipped back and forth between the shots of her clients with and without their masks, then scanned the crowd again.

On her left were five familiar costumes. Four of her guests and Tom were grouped together at the back of the hall, chatting animatedly.

Lana breathed a sigh of relief. Tom did seem a bit too self-assured at times, and she was still not certain whether he would hit it off with their predominantly wealthy guests. Considering he had been leading tours for years in Central and South America, she figured he had the right to feel confident in his abilities. However, he still seemed a bit rough around the edges and more used to leading the pack than going along for the ride.

"What a party. Are all the Wanderlust tours so luxurious?" Tom asked after Lana joined them. As smug as he may be, he did look ravishing in his green waistcoat with silver accents embroidered onto the sleeves.

"I wish," she laughed. "This is definitely the high point for me, after a year and a half of guiding."

"That's right, you're still pretty new at this," Tom replied in a casual tone. Lana figured he didn't mean his words to sound degrading, but they still stung.

"It's a gown, not a dress," Kathy, said, her words slightly slurred as she lay a hand on Tom's forearm. "Aren't they fabulous? I'm so glad you knew of a costume shop we could rent these at. I feel like a queen in this thing!"

"Truth be told, that was Matteo's doing. He set up the appointment with the rental shop for us before we left Seattle," Lana replied.

"That sounds about right," Dave said, the tone of his voice exposing his bitterness. "Matteo does seem to love to micromanage everything and everyone. Well, except his accounting department, apparently."

"How are you enjoying the evening so far?" Lana asked, when she noticed Dave's darkening tone. She shifted her body as she spoke, directing the words at all of her guests. "Have you danced yet? Or should I say waltzed?"

"We aren't really party people," Harry answered. "But this ball is incredible. Sail Away Cruises spared no expense to send Matteo off."

"What do you mean?" Lana asked. "I thought this was to celebrate his being CEO for twenty years. I didn't realize he was retiring."

"It's not explicitly a retirement party, I'll give you that. But according to Sail Away's board of directors," Harry said, nodding towards a group of men dressed in jester masks standing close by, "Matteo has sworn for years that he would retire after twenty years, just as his predecessor did, and give the next generation a shot. He sees it as his duty to the company. They already have his successor prepped and waiting in the wings."

"How exciting! This puts a whole new spin on the evening," Lana said. In fact, she was greatly relieved to hear that he was stepping down. The low point of the evening so far had been meeting the man of honor. Matteo came across as an overly macho bully, the kind who probably thought it was funny to slap his female co-workers on the backside or call them "honey." It was indeed time for men like that to move aside and give the younger generation a chance to shine.

"It certainly does," Harry exclaimed, a wide grin splitting his face. He put a thick hand on his brother's shoulder and squeezed. "I think we deserve another beer to celebrate."

"Great idea," Joe responded. "Can we get anyone else another drink?" He looked to his bosses.

"Another prosecco, please. They are so delicious," Kathy giggled.

"Since you are offering, I could use another beer," Dave said.

"Me, too," Tom said.

Lana wanted to slap her hand against her forehead. Tom should have known better than to ask a guest to grab him a drink. On the other hand, maybe that was normal on the backpacker-style trips his former employer offered. The line between guide and client sounded far more vague than on those sold by Wanderlust. And Tom had been hanging around with Harry and Joe so much, he might feel more like their friends than their guide. It was a line that was easily crossed, and one guides were warned to guard against. As nice as a tourist may be, or as well as a guide may get on with them, Dotty asked everyone to maintain a professional distance with all of their guests while the tour was going on.

She looked to Tom, wondering how she could say something without her guests noticing, when he added, "That's a lot of drinks. Why don't I help you carry them back?"

Phew, she thought. Maybe he wasn't as clueless as she had feared.

"Back in a minute," Harry said and the three men walked off towards the bar.

"We will have to show our appreciation more often," Kathy said once the brothers were out of earshot. "Those two have never been so even-tempered!"

"True," Dave responded, his tone more reflective. "Though sometimes I think that their explosive temperament is simply a way of covering up their quest for perfection. They are true craftsmen."

Lana swore she saw the man blink away a tear.

Kathy rolled her eyes and opened her mouth, but before she could respond, an elegantly dressed woman in her late thirties drifted over and curtsied. The stranger's costume was even more elaborate than those Lana's group had rented, and it seemed to be tailored to the woman's tiny waist and large bustline. She wore a burgundy-colored mask decorated with glitter, shimmering stones, and several feathers. A shiny red scarf covered her hair.

The lady raised her mask and winked. "Hello, Dave and Kathy. I'm Vittoria Russo, and I'm so glad to see you here."

"Vittoria! It is great to finally meet you in person. We can't wait to discuss our future plans together," Dave said, pumping her hand as he spoke.

Lana recognized the woman's name as that of the senior vice president of Sail Away Cruises.

"It will be an honor to work with you. Matteo always favored the mega-ships, but I want to shift our focus to smaller ships and a more luxurious experience. Your ships are masterpieces and exactly what I want the future fleets of Sail Away Cruises to look like," she purred.

"See, what did I tell you?" Dave said to his wife. "There's nothing to worry about."

Kathy chuckled and looked away, clearly embarrassed by her husband's choice of words.

A young woman in a wide ball gown approached rapidly. Her mask was hanging off her wrist, and her hair was coming loose from the bun piled up on top of her head. A pair of reading glasses sat crooked on the edge of her nose. It was Bianca, Matteo's assistant, Lana realized. She started to raise her mask to say hello, when Bianca turned to Vittoria.

"Have you seen Matteo? Two investors want to speak with him."

"I'm not his keeper—you are. Besides, Matteo is old news. If it has anything to do with Sail Away Cruises, then they would do better to talk directly to me."

The young woman seemed to waffle, before adding, "Alright, but I think they want to congratulate Matteo. The party is being held in his honor, after all."

"He was at the bar the last time that I saw him," Vittoria said in a dismissive tone.

Before Bianca could take a step, a deep voice boomed from across the hall. "Bianca? It's time."

Vittoria's eyebrows shot up as she smirked at Matteo's assistant. "What a surprise—he found you first."

Bianca's mouth formed a sneer, but before she could retort, Matteo called out again.

His assistant tensed up. "I better go to him before he starts to yell. Matteo does have a short temper."

After Bianca walked off, Vittoria snickered. "Bianca has to be his worst assistant, yet. That girl couldn't find a shoe if it was on her foot. I wonder what she's holding over him."

Before Lana could ask what she meant, Matteo's voice reached them again. "Vittoria, I need you over here."

The vice president's expression darkened. "If you will excuse me, I have to go see what my boss needs." She paused and laughed, before lowering her mask and walking away. "It will be nice not to have to say that again."

"What did she mean, do you think?" Lana asked.

"Vittoria is the successor the board has been grooming," Dave said. "I bet she is counting the minutes until Matteo announces his retirement."

6

Storm Ahead

Curious to see whether the others were enjoying the party, Lana took out her phone and glanced at the costumes the rest of her clients were wearing. She immediately spotted Carmen and Rhonda standing close to the buffet. Chrissy and George were by the bar, chatting with another couple. Lana flipped a mental coin in her head before turning towards the pair of widowed friends. However, before she could reach them, the lights blinked and a deep voice boomed over the loud speaker. "Welcome, all!"

The source was Matteo Conti, a short, broad man who appeared to be in his late sixties. His ruddy skin and many wrinkles made it difficult to judge his age. After he climbed up onto a makeshift podium in the corner of the hall, a spotlight zeroed in on him. Once in position, he smiled warmly and opened his arms to the crowd.

"Ladies and gentlemen, it is wonderful to see so many friendly faces here tonight to help me celebrate two decades as CEO of Sail Away Cruises. Leading this company for so long has been my greatest honor."

The applause, cheers, and whistles were almost deafening. Lana clapped along, impressed by the audience's reaction. But then again, from what Dotty had told her, all of the invitees either worked for or with Sail Away Cruises. After twenty years, Matteo had obviously built up a massive network.

Lana gently worked her way through the room, reaching her clients as the applause died down. Carmen and Rhonda smiled at Lana just as Matteo continued.

"As many of you know, I started working for Sail Away Cruises right after I finished high school. I joined the company as a deckhand and slowly worked my way up through the ranks, all the way to the top! When my predecessor retired twenty years ago, he gave me a special gift to commemorate the occasion. Ah, here it is."

Matteo shifted his gaze to the back of the hall, where the vice president was now descending a flight of stairs. As she walked towards her boss, a spotlight lit up her path. The object in her hands sparkled under the bright light, capturing everyone's attention.

Appreciative murmurs arose from the crowd as Vittoria passed through. Lana stood on her toes to better see what everyone was getting excited about. It was a golden statue of a gondola, about as long as the vice president's forearm. Embedded in the boat's hull were several rows of jewels that danced in the lights as she moved through the crowd.

"Ah, here it is—my pride and joy. Thanks, Vittoria."

The vice president smiled warmly at Matteo as she handed her boss the gondola.

Matteo took ahold of it by its marble base and raised it up high, turning it in the spotlight and causing the precious stones to sparkle.

A mousy man in a bow tie and corduroy jacket stepped forward and appeared to try and touch the gondola. Matteo took two steps back, too far for the man to reach the statue without joining him up on stage. The strange little man responded by turning to face the crowd and spreading out his arms, as if he was a velvet rope.

Vittoria also stayed close to Matteo, standing to the right of the podium as she looked up to her boss with an adoring gaze. Standing in her shadow was Matteo's assistant, Bianca.

"This simple gondola was crafted in the nineteenth century as a souvenir for tourists, though this one is quite a bit bigger and heavier than those that can be found in contemporary gift shops, let me assure you."

Vittoria began to laugh, and the audience chuckled along.

"This gondola rests on the table in the center of my living room, as a constant reminder of what I've achieved. At the end of each year, I had a jewel added to its hull. These precious stones remind me of all that I have already accomplished, and the empty spaces symbolize the work yet to come." Matteo's voice was melancholy as he gazed at the little boat in his hand. Lana could imagine it would be difficult to retire after successfully leading an international company for twenty years.

"That thing is gawdy with a capital G," Carmen whispered to her traveling companion.

Lana stifled a chuckle.

"I bet I could get twenty grand for it. Maybe thirty if I found the right client," Rhonda replied in an equally soft voice.

Lana's laugh became a cough. She knew that Rhonda owned an antiques and collectibles business, but that seemed to be an astronomically high amount for a rather ugly statue. "Is it really worth that much or are you a great saleswoman?"

"If those jewels are genuine, and the gondola is really nineteenth century, then it's worth at least that much," Rhonda replied.

When Lana looked at her guest skeptically, Carmen patted her arm. "Her estimate may sound high, but Rhonda has an incredible eye and has been in the business for decades. I would trust her appraisal."

Matteo's voice boomed over the microphone, redirecting their attention to the podium. "The rubies, emeralds, and pearls that I have had added for each year as CEO have increased its value substantially. Which is why I said that when I retired, I would donate it to a local museum, as a way of thanking this great city for providing me a wonderful life and career."

When Matteo stared at the statue in hand, Lana swore she saw him blink away a tear. Moments later, he bowed to the mousy man still standing guard in front of the podium, who returned the gesture. "Unfortunately, my friend, that time has not come."

The museum representative's face grew ashen as Matteo continued on. Vittoria's adoring expression also turned to confusion.

"Times are changing fast, as the new laws regulating Venice's waters exemplify. Sail Away needs a strong leader at its helm to guide us through these rough waters, and the best person for the job is still me."

A wave of gasps emanated from the crowd. Apparently the Windsor crew weren't the only ones expecting Mateo to announce his retirement. Lana looked over to the group of bigwigs Harry had pointed out and noticed they all seemed to be in a state of panic. Could Mateo simply decide that he was staying on, or did the board of directors need to approve his request?

"The new year will bring new routes and partnerships." Mateo nodded to a well-dressed man standing close to the podium, who bowed slightly in acknowledgment. "Because of the changes in regulations, I have decided to reduce our Venice fleet and focus our attention on river cruises. Thanks to my connections, we will be working with one of the most prestigious boat builders based in Europe, which incidentally will save us thousands in taxes and transportation costs," Mateo said, his hand up to his mouth, as if he was whispering a secret into the microphone.

"Why, you!" a woman shrieked from the back of the hall. Lana looked towards the source, but couldn't see who had spoken. All of the expressionless masks made it impossible to know who had yelled out and were a strange, unsettling sight. Yet, the voice did sound familiar.

"Kathy, stop! Wait until he's done, then we confront him," Lana heard Dave say.

Oh, no, Lana thought. Did that mean that Sail Away wasn't going to pay for the Windsors' boats, after all? It sure sounded like it. If that was what Mateo was implying, then she could imagine Dave and Kathy were livid right now, especially at hearing the news in such a public way.

Mateo paused and stared out over the packed hall. "I know that I have always said I would step aside after twenty years, just as my predecessor did. Yet, now that that day is here, I see no reason to stop. I am in perfect health, I love my job, and my leadership continues to help our company grow. It's not yet my time to retire and sail off into the sunset. Which is why I have decided to stay on for another five years."

Mateo turned his attention back to the statue in his hand. "My jeweler is going to have a heck of a time adding five more stones. I might just have to have another gondola made."

His attempt at a joke received more gasps than chuckles from his audience.

"Are you certain that staying on another five years is a good idea?" a male voice called out. Lana's money was on a member of the board of directors, but in this crowd it was impossible to know for certain.

"Why not? I have a lot of life in me yet!" Matteo replied. "Now my friends, let us eat, drink, and be merry. Thanks again for coming to my party. Enjoy your night!"

7

Lost in Translation

As soon as the smattering of applause died down, the museum representative stepped up onto the podium and began cursing Matteo out in Italian.

"What is going on there?" Lana wondered aloud.

"He is flaming mad that Matteo is delaying the handover. Apparently the museum already paid for a professional cleaning and some minor restoration work," Carmen said, shrugging when Lana looked at her inquisitively. "I was an art historian and curator specializing in Renaissance art—it was handy to be fluent in Italian and French."

Matteo pleaded with the man, grinning while he did.

"Matteo is telling him to have patience, his museum will still get the gondola, in due time. But our museum friend is not happy and is going to tell his boss. And now he is warning Matteo that he should expect a call from their lawyers."

Seconds later, the museum representative stormed off towards the exit.

Rhonda turned to her friend. "As much as I'm enjoying the party, I am rather pooped out. I wouldn't mind leaving, either. How are you doing, Carmen?"

Lana looked to her watch and noted that it was already eleven.

Carmen nodded. "I wouldn't mind hitting the sack. We do have a busy day tomorrow."

"Shall I escort you ladies outside then? They should have a taxi stand next to the entrance."

"That would be lovely, but I would like to use the facilities before we go," Rhonda said. "Carmen, would you join me? We'll meet you back here in a minute."

"Of course." Lana smiled. "Take your time."

As soon as the pair walked away, Matteo passed by, swerving slightly as he went. The alcohol had been flowing all night, and the man of honor had clearly had his fair share. Lana began to follow, gently pushing her wide skirt through the thick crowd. Despite his behavior, she had promised Dotty that she would thank him for booking with Wanderlust Tours and inviting the entire group to the party.

Lana had almost caught up with him, when the Fretwells crossed his path first.

"George! Good to see you, old man. I see life is still being good to you," Matteo said, pointing to George's ample belly.

"They do say a way to a man's heart is through his stomach. And my wife is an excellent cook," George joked as he patted his midriff.

He pulled Chrissy closer and kissed her on the cheek. Lana was shocked to see that his wife was doing all she could to avoid Matteo's gaze. The CEO must have noticed, as well. Matteo offered her a hand as he bowed in front of her, making it impossible for Chrissy to ignore him without coming across as rude.

"Ah, yes, the lovely Chrissy. I haven't seen you since I flew over to Seattle— what was that, two years ago? It is too bad you were not able to attend last year's ball, but I am honored to see you here tonight."

"Yeah, well, I didn't have a choice," she muttered, garnering shocked expressions from both her husband and Matteo.

"Chrissy, why are you being so rude?" her husband whispered. She only shook her head and looked away.

Before either man could respond, Carmen tapped on Lana's shoulder. "We are ready to go when you are."

Lana turned to her clients, wishing they had been a few minutes longer, and smiled broadly. "Alright! Let's find you a taxi."

She helped the two ladies navigate back outside and through the rows of protesters, still being restrained by columns of burly security guards. The number of activists and signs advocating a boycott of Sail Away Cruises seemed to have grown since the party started.

"It is good that young people let their opinion be known," Carmen said, nodding at the crowd in approval.

Lana got her clients down to the water's edge and onto the floating platform without incident, where several others were already waiting for more water taxis, or *vaporetti*, to arrive. She loved the fact that, in Venice, the waterways were the major transportation networks, not roads.

Standing in line before them was the representative from the local museum, the one who had expected to leave the party with Matteo's gondola statue. He still seemed to be simmering mad as he spat into his telephone.

"My, my, he does have a temper," Carmen whispered. "It seems that the museum had already ordered a display case for the gondola, and had renamed the hall after Matteo. He's going to the director's home now, so they can call the museum's legal team. I'm afraid they are going to have a long and unpleasant night, instead of the joyous one they were expecting."

"You shouldn't count your eggs before they hatch, as my father loved to say," Rhonda replied in a soft voice.

The threesome did their best to ignore the museum representative and enjoy the glorious views. The bridges and many buildings were lit up with tiny spotlights, making it seem as if the structures glowed in the moonlight. Despite the late hour, the waters were busy with watercraft, the majority of which were taxis shuttling customers from parties to hotels, and back again. From their low vantage point, Lana could see the blue-green water swirling in the boats' wakes.

After what seemed like an hour, several empty taxis pulled up to the platform and ferried all but their group and the museum representative away. It took another ten minutes for the next boat to arrive, by which time, Rhonda was shivering in the slight breeze.

"I knew I should have brought a wrap for the ride home, but it was such a warm evening I thought I could get away without one."

Carmen rubbed her friend's bare arms. "It looks like another taxi is arriving. Why don't we ask the museum guy if we can share it?"

"Can you do it, Carmen? He seems pretty keyed up," Rhonda said through chattering teeth.

"I'll ask him," Lana offered, knowing it was her duty to do so. The *vaporetto* pulled up to platform, spraying water up as the captain reversed the engines.

When the museum representative finished his call and stepped towards the boat, Lana cleared her throat. "Excuse me, sir, but it's rather chilly and we have no way of knowing when the next taxi will arrive. Could we please share this ride?"

The museum representative shook his head. "I have no time for delays," he said before springing into the boat. He barked something in Italian at the captain, and the boat's motor roared to life.

"That's a no," Carmen quipped as the boat sped off into the night. "Oh, well, another one will be along soon. There is no sense in you catching a cold, as well, Lana. Why don't you head back inside? We can manage."

Lana stayed put. Before Carmen could insist, another taxi approached the dock. After she helped them in, she waved at her guests. "Take care, ladies. I'll see you in the morning."

"Thanks! Enjoy the rest of the party," Rhonda called out as the boat pulled away from the dock.

That's exactly what I intend to do, Lana thought, as she skipped back upstairs.

8

Batten Down the Hatches

When Lana re-entered the hall, the magic she had initially felt was slightly tempered by the angry shouts echoing through the space. The source was Matteo, the man of honor.

"Why can't you just do what I tell you to?" he raged.

His current victim was Vittoria Russo. The poor woman was probably still reeling from Matteo's announcement that he was going to stay on for another five years. *You would think that he would give Vittoria a break, tonight of all nights*, Lana thought. He must have been aware of how his decision to stay on would impact her.

The two were facing each other and, based on their expressions, neither was willing to back down.

Vittoria had Matteo's golden gondola in her hands. "Why can't your assistant do it?" she grumbled.

"You are both my subordinates, so it really doesn't matter which one of you puts the gondola back in my office's safe."

Based on their body language, this argument was a show of power, not just a tiff about the statue.

"Why did you lie to keep me here?" Vittoria asked.

Matteo took a step closer to her and squared his shoulders. "I can't have you competing against me, can I?"

Although he was obviously trying to intimidate Vittoria, his tactics did not work. They only seemed to incense her further. "I am the senior vice president of Sail Away Cruises, not your servant. I have put up with your sexist remarks and appalling behavior for far too long. I have half a mind to throw this thing off the roof."

"You break it, you pay for it," Matteo growled. "And trust me, your current salary won't be enough to cover the repairs."

Vittoria began to retort, yet when she noticed that the entire hall was watching them bicker, she turned on her heel and retreated upstairs with the gondola in hand.

Seconds later, the Windsors took her place.

"You lied to us! Our ships aren't built for river cruises," Kathy screamed, right in Matteo's face.

"Is that why you are trying to get out of paying us for the ships you ordered?" Dave asked. "Are you really working with one of our competitors now?"

"Who let you in?" Matteo barked, ignoring their questions. "You aren't welcome here."

"You uninvited us?" Dave asked, disbelief in his voice. "But why? We did everything you asked, yet you have not responded to any of our recent emails or phone calls, and you still have not paid the rest of the invoice. And now you tell us we aren't welcome at your party? What is going on?"

"You were three months too late, and your boats are too long."

Dave and Kathy's faces drained of color. "That's not true. They are two hundred meters, as you requested. You even called us after the changes were announced and assured us that the new law would not impact the order," Dave insisted.

Instead of answering, Matteo screamed, "Bianca!"

Seconds later, his assistant appeared by his side. "Yes?"

"You messed up again! I've had enough. I don't care who your father is, you're out. Tomorrow morning at eight a.m. sharp, I want to see you in my office. It's time to talk about your future here, or lack thereof."

"But I did cancel their tickets! I even called Wanderlust Tours to confirm they had received my emails about it."

Lana thought back to what Dotty had told her about this trip. Sail Away

Cruises had purchased six of the ten places on this tour as gifts for the Fretwells, the Windsors, and another couple of investors who were unable to come because the wife broke her hip. The Windsors had purchased two more, as gifts for Harry and Joe. Carmen and Rhonda had snatched up the last two places, filling the tour months before the departure date.

Months later, when Bianca sent several emails and then called Wanderlust Tours to explain that Sail Away Cruises only wished to pay for four of the six tickets, Dotty told the young woman that she understood the request, but refused to cancel the reservations, on principle. Dotty argued that the clients had already received their hotel and airline tickets and that it was bad for business to tell them that they were not allowed to use them anymore, especially when she could not explain why.

"Apparently you didn't make yourself clear enough because they are standing here at my party."

"But Vittoria said—"

"Enough! Stop shifting the blame to others and take responsibility for your actions, for once. You really are the worst assistant I have ever had, and that's saying something."

Bianca slunk away, wiping at the river of tears already cascading down her cheeks.

Lana's heart went out to the young woman. "Excuse me, but there seems to be a misunderstanding. Two weeks before our departure date, Bianca did call and ask us to cancel the Windsors' reservations. But it was too late to get a refund on any of the hotel rooms or plane tickets and Dotty did not feel that it was her place to tell the Windsors that the tickets they had already been issued were no longer valid," Lana explained, trying to keep the tremor out of her voice.

Matteo turned on her, his face a mask of pure rage. "You can tell your boss that this is the last time Sail Away will be using her services."

Great going, Lana, she thought, wishing she had kept her mouth shut. Now she had to explain to Dotty how she had lost Wanderlust Tours an important client.

Matteo turned his sights back onto Dave and Kathy. "Why are you still here?"

"You assured us that the length was not a problem, even after the recent change in laws, thanks to your connections!" Kathy screamed, her voice echoing around the now-silent hall. Pretty much everyone present had stopped to watch their verbal fight escalate.

"You must have misunderstood me," Matteo replied in an equally loud voice as he turned to address the crowded room. "I don't bribe people, despite the recent rumors carelessly reprinted in the local newspapers, claiming the contrary. The new law states that an ocean-going vessel must be one hundred and eighty meters or less in length, in order to sail into the Venice Basin. Yours are twenty meters too long."

"Why didn't you cancel the contract as soon as the laws changed, instead of ordering more pricy additions to the ships we were building?"

"Because I was trying to find a way to incorporate them into another line, so as to honor our contract, but it proved impossible. As you pointed out, they are ocean-going vessels that we currently have no need for. Since I cannot use them, I am not going to pay for them. And it is entirely legal, thanks to the clause in our contract."

Dave and Kathy were shaking with anger. "It's too late to change your mind now—the boats have been built to your specifications! You're just looking for an excuse to get out of the contract. We'll go bankrupt if you invoke that clause!"

"That's not my problem." Matteo smirked and began to turn away.

"Our lawyer is going to love hearing that joke you made about the taxes. I bet the judge will take your insinuations into consideration, regardless of the clause."

"Tell you what, why don't we let our lawyers deal with this? It's a waste of a good party to fight during it. Since you're here, have a beer on me." His amicable tone only made things worse.

When he reached out to pat Dave on the back, the American man slapped Matteo's arm away and lunged at him. "You arrogant jerk!"

Harry and Joe grabbed their boss's arms and pulled him away.

Matteo began to retort, but apparently thought better of it. Instead, he turned on his heel, smiling as if nothing had happened, and strode off towards the bar, leaving the rest gaping after him.

"Is he even aware of what a monster he is? Does he care what happens to anyone who works for him?" Kathy asked her husband, wiping tears from her eyes. "Who else is going to want his over-the-top cruise ships?"

"I don't know what to think. I know I could use a drink," Dave said as he looked over to the bar. "But I'll wait until the man of honor has gotten his and moved on."

Lana followed his eyes, spotting Matteo standing at the front of the line. Seconds later, he received a drink and moved to the end of the bar where Chrissy was standing, sipping a cocktail as she watched the party. He moved towards her, swaying as he walked, and without warning, placed his hand firmly on Chrissy's backside.

Chrissy jerked away, splashing her drink onto his shirt when she turned to curse Matteo out. Lana couldn't hear her words, but it was clear that Matteo's hand was uninvited. Chrissy began to walk off when Matteo grabbed her arm and pulled her back towards him. Lana's skin crawled as she watched his lecherous behavior. Concerned for her client's safety, she raced across the crowded hall, hoping reach them before this situation escalated.

"What's your problem? You weren't so cold in Seattle," Matteo said as Lana approached the pair.

"Leave me alone!" Chrissy cried out. Unfortunately, no one standing near the pair seemed to want to intervene.

When Chrissy raised her other hand to slap him, Matteo grabbed both of her wrists and pulled her hands to his lips. "Come now," he purred as he tried to nuzzle his head into her neck.

George reached them before Lana could. "Get your hands off of my wife!" he screamed and dragged Matteo away from Chrissy.

Instead of blushing and letting her go, Matteo kissed her fingertips before releasing her wrists. "I'll see you upstairs," he whispered, far too loudly. Everyone within earshot could easily hear him.

"What is going on here?" George asked, his expression livid.

"Nothing! He must be drunk and got grabby, but his advances were not invited," Chrissy wept.

"It wouldn't be the first time," George growled, causing her to blush. "What did he mean about Seattle?"

"I truly don't know," Chrissy cried. She was shaking so much the purple stones hanging off her new necklace jangled against each other.

"After all the money that I've dumped into his company, he shows his respect by hitting on my wife? I'm pulling all of my money out of Sail Away Cruises tonight. Where did that slimeball run off to? We're going to sort this out, here and now," George yelled.

Vittoria rushed over and blocked his path. "Wait! Please don't make any rash decisions. Matteo is not a dictator, despite his posturing tonight. The board of directors has the last say as to who runs Sail Away Cruises. You'll have to trust me when I say that I'll be running things before you know it."

"I don't care who does what. All I know is that no one embarrasses me like that and gets away with it." George puffed up his chest and gently pushed Vittoria aside. "Now, where is he?"

She pointed towards the stairwell. "In his office. I believe he is waiting for your wife to join him."

She turned on her heel as George turned beet red and ran towards the stairs.

Thanks for throwing fuel on the fire, Vittoria, Lana fumed. *What do I do now?*

From what she could tell, George, Chrissy and Matteo had all drunk so much alcohol tonight that none of them were thinking clearly.

Tom came up behind her and whispered, "Should we go after him?"

Lana thought a moment before shaking her head. "Marital problems don't qualify as a tour-related issue, at least not in my book. They are all adults. I think it's best if we stay out of it."

Before Tom could respond, a scuffle at the other end of the hall caught their attention.

"Uh, oh. What are they doing?" he asked.

The Windsor crew had surrounded the competing boat builder that Matteo had mentioned during his speech.

"Are you trying to steal our contract? The ten ships Matteo ordered were supposed to be the first of many. You do know that he still hasn't paid us, don't you?"

"Why should he pay your overinflated prices when he can buy mine for half the cost? We signed a contract for twenty riverboats just last week. He has already paid me every dime he owed me," the man sneered.

"I knew it! Matteo was never going to pay the rest of his invoice," Dave cried as he looked around the hall. "Where is that liar? I want to have a word with him."

Tom leaned in closer to Lana but kept his eyes locked on the escalating squabble. "Does this qualify as our territory, or should we continue to stay out of it?"

Lana looked to her guests, slightly disgusted with their behavior, when Harry and Dave suddenly stormed off towards the staircase leading up to the upper floor offices. "You know what, they are all adults. They can take care of themselves."

The tiffs had sapped the last of her energy, and suddenly Lana felt like going back to the hotel. She glanced around the hall and estimated that more than half of the guests had already left. Those who remained were hanging around the bar, enjoying the free drinks.

Standing at one end of the bar was Chrissy, slamming shots. *If she keeps that up, she won't be able to walk out of here*, Lana thought as she went to her client.

"Are you alright, Chrissy?"

"Not really. Could you call me a taxi? I want to go back to the hotel."

"Sure, but do you want to wait for George?"

"No way! I have no desire to see Matteo again. I'll text George and let him know where I'm at."

"Alright, I'll walk out to the taxi stand with you. Give me a minute to let Tom know where I've gone. I'll be right back." Lana scurried off, shaking her head when she saw Chrissy raise her finger to order another drink.

She crossed over to her fellow guide, currently chatting up a dark-haired beauty. "Sorry to interrupt, but Chrissy wants to go back to the hotel and I am going to join her."

"Oh, okay. Should I leave, as well?" Tom asked.

"Heavens, no—enjoy yourself. But just so you know, this party is not a normal occurrence on a Wanderlust tour. I don't want you to think they are all this fancy."

Tom laughed. "I'll keep that in mind. I'm going to stay a while longer, then. Have a good night."

Lana left him to his date and returned to the bar, but Chrissy was nowhere to be seen. She checked the taxi stand, yet didn't see her client waiting on the now-empty pontoon. *Chrissy is an adult,* Lana reasoned. *If she got herself down to the taxi stand, then she must be doing better than I thought.*

She waffled between taking a taxi back, or walking, until she noticed how the lights sparkled on the dark water. Couples kissed and cuddled as they strolled along the tiny streets. Lana turned down a taxi ride, choosing to walk back to her hotel, instead. *Why not, I'm in no rush,* she thought.

The party was winding down, and Tom was still there in case their clients needed help getting down to the taxi stand. What could possibly go wrong?

9

Missing Alex

Lana took a detour back to her hotel, reveling in the magnificent views. Rialto Bridge was brightly lit, its distinctive single-arch design and covered arcade clearly defined in the moonless night. Several wooden poles sticking out of the water served as piers for gondolas and other small watercraft, tied up with a simple rope. A devilish streak went through Lana, as she contemplated jumping into one of the gondolas, if only to experience how it felt to sit inside of one. At more than a hundred dollars a pop, she didn't see herself booking a gondola ride anytime soon.

Venice was gorgeous at any time of the day, but at night the city seemed even more magical. The darkened alleyways, bridges that seemed to disappear into the darkness, and the dramatically lit Gothic architecture were mysterious, yet inviting. For some reason, Lana didn't feel scared walking these streets at this late hour, even in her medieval gown, a Carnevale mask hanging off her arm. Somehow the knowledge that there were so many tourists still milling about was comforting. Someone would surely come to her aid, if she needed assistance.

She passed the entrance to her hotel twice, not yet ready to call it a night. The city's many canals kept beckoning her back. Lights flickered from lanterns hanging off of a few gondolas' bows, the sleek boats otherwise invisible in the dark water. A few water taxis motored past, their seats sparsely filled with late-night partygoers. Every bridge was illuminated with hundreds of bulbs that danced and sparkled in the churning water.

Lana stopped by the canal's edge and watched two lovers kissing as their gondola floated by. The gondolier's singing reminded her of Harry's surprise performance earlier in the day. *The only thing that would make this night more perfect would be having Alex here with me.*

As she approached her hotel for a third time, the sound of fast-approaching sirens made her heart accelerate. She looked towards the water and saw a string of blue and white boats, the word *"polizia"* adorning their sides. They raced by at astounding speeds, their lights ablaze, and their wake splashed high up over the canal walls. When they continued on past her hotel, Lana breathed a sigh of relief. They weren't looking for her tour group. After months of being continually confronted with death on her tours, Lana was really looking forward to a fatality-free trip.

They must be going to arrest the protesters, she realized as the column of boats turned in the direction of Sail Away Cruises' headquarters. It had certainly seemed like the later it got, the rowdier the activists got.

As she entered her hotel, one of her heels got caught in the carpet and her shoe flew off, completing her vision of being Cinderella for the evening. Luckily for her, midnight had come and gone, but nothing around her had turned into a pumpkin.

Lana plucked her shoe off the floor and pulled off the other, giggling as she did. When she stepped into an awaiting elevator, she could hardly believe how lucky she felt. Day four of their tour was about to conclude without a hint of murder or serious mayhem. Perhaps the curse that seemed to have followed her recent tours around Europe had finally lifted.

After she entered her room and threw open the balcony doors, the strong breeze sent the intricately woven curtains billowing into the room. Even at one in the morning, the air was warm. She leaned against the wrought-iron balcony and gazed out at the beautifully illuminated palazzos on the opposite side and sighed deeply, feeling intensely happy.

When a group of boisterous tourists on the street below began to sing loudly, Lana closed the balcony doors and flipped on the television before shimmying out of her dress. A woman with a high-pitched voice was pitching a hand soap. As Lana pulled one of the hotel's fluffy bathrobes around her, rapid-fire Italian filled the room. She glanced at the screen and, based on the images, guessed that the local news was starting. Lana returned to the bathroom and pulled out the many clips she had used to keep her hair up. She was massaging her scalp when the Italian news presenter's voice rose an octave and increased in speed.

Though she didn't understand the language, the intensity with which he spoke drew her back to the screen. A series of short videos and photos told the story of a break-in that had just taken place at Sail Away Cruises' headquarters.

"What the?" Lana cried out when the building in which the masquerade ball was still taking place came into view. She grabbed the remote control and flipped to the BBC, hoping that whatever was happening was important enough to be covered internationally. Her bet paid off. The BBC was showing the same videos she had just seen, but with English-language commentary.

"Several members of the radical protest group Earth Warriors were arrested in Venice last night after breaking into the offices of Sail Away Cruises. The company was throwing a party two floors below, to celebrate Matteo Conti's twenty years as CEO. Moments ago, Mr. Conti was also found dead in his office, though details are sketchy as to how the two crimes are related. Stay tuned for more updates as we follow this breaking story."

Matteo was dead? Lana sat down heavily on her hotel room bed, staring at the screen with wide eyes. "The party was only two floors down. Why didn't any of us hear anything going on?" she wondered aloud.

Then again, an orchestra or choir had been performing all night long, and the noise of the large crowd was quite intense. The protesters could have broken a window on the upper floors, and no one at the party would have heard them.

She cast her mind back to the masquerade ball, trying to recall when she had seen Matteo last. He had gone up to his office after getting into arguments with Vittoria, George, Chrissy, and the Windsor crew. And those were only the verbal fights that she had witnessed. Given his dominating personality and heavy alcohol consumption, Lana suspected Matteo had angered other partygoers with his belligerent behavior tonight.

She couldn't recall seeing Matteo coming back down from his office before she left the party. Which was, in fact, only minutes after he had gone upstairs to wait for Chrissy. Had she joined him, after all? Or had Chrissy taken a taxi back to the hotel?

My guests! Lana suddenly realized the Windsor crew and George were still there. Luckily, Tom had stayed behind. If the police were to question those still at the party, hopefully he would stick around long enough to ensure all of their guests made it back to the hotel after they were released.

Lana's pulse accelerated when the British news reader held a finger to his ear and listened. When he turned his attention back to the camera, his tone was even more somber. "The police have confirmed that the suspected killer is also a member of Earth Warriors and that he had fled the scene before they arrived. Witnesses saw him fleeing towards the Strada Nova. Police are actively searching the area for the suspect and ask all those in the center of Venice to remain indoors until he has been apprehended."

"That's really close by," Lana mumbled, recalling that she'd walked along the Strada Nova to reach her hotel's entrance. However, it was quite a long street that wound its way past several high-end hotels and restaurants. It was probably a coincidence.

When she opened her balcony doors again, the scream of police sirens was immediately audible. The longer she listened, the louder they became. She stepped out onto the balcony as a fleet of police boats pulled up to the canal's edge. When she looked to the right, she noted several officers were already weaving through the masses of tourists filling the street.

A hard knock on her door pulled Lana back into the room. Figuring it was one of her guests worried about the police presence on the streets below, she knotted her bathrobe's cord and put on a confident smile before answering.

"What can I do for you?" Her face fell as she took in the sight before her. "Alex?"

Her boyfriend was standing in the doorway, his ripped pants and torn shirt splattered with blood.

"Oh, Lana. No matter what anyone says, I did not kill that man."

10

In Deep Water

"You are supposed to be in Berlin," Lana muttered as her body tilted back against the open door.

Alex grabbed her shoulders and gently pushed her back into the room. After closing the door behind them, he cradled her face with his hands. "I am so sorry for dragging you into this, my love, but I didn't know where else to turn."

He leaned forward to kiss her, but suddenly pulled back, his eyes wide. "Oh, no—your face," Alex moaned and stared at his hands. "We'd better wash up."

Lana let out a tiny shriek when she touched her cheek and her fingertip came back red.

"Why you are covered in blood? It's still wet, Alex. What is going on?" She followed him into the bathroom, stopping short when she caught a glimpse of herself in the mirror. Her hotel's complimentary bathrobe looked like a butcher had borrowed it. The once pristine white terry cloth was now covered with splotches of blood that seemed to grow in size the longer Lana looked at them.

"Ewww!" She tore the bloody bathrobe off and switched it out for a clean one.

Alex sighed as he hung his head low. "It's not what it looks like. Most of it is pig blood."

"But not all of it?" Lana washed her face twice with soap, scrubbing until her skin felt raw.

Alex refused to meet her gaze while he dried off his hands, arms, and face. After he'd finished, he stared into the mirror for a long minute, before finally turning to face his girlfriend. When they locked eyes, she could see that his were bloodshot.

"I have so much to explain to you, but let's stick with what's most important for the moment. I promise I'll tell you everything once we get through this."

Lana's eyes narrowed as her mind raced through the reasons why her boyfriend would be covered in blood—pig or otherwise. "Okay, Let's start with a simple question. Whose blood is it?"

"I'm not sure," Alex mumbled.

"You aren't sure? How do you get blood all over you and not know whose it is?"

Alex tore at his hair. "Because I didn't kill that man! I didn't know his body was in there when I went inside!"

Lana's heart was racing faster than the engine of a Formula One race car. "Inside where, Alex? You are scaring me. Can you slow down and explain yourself better?"

"You better sit down." He motioned towards the two chairs next to the bed and waited for her to choose a seat before joining her.

"We broke into the headquarters of Sail Away Cruises tonight with the intention of trashing the senior staff members' offices and hanging a protest banner out of the window."

Lana shook her head, certain she had misheard her boyfriend. "Let's back up a minute. Were you one of the activists protesting by the entrance? When did you join Earth Warriors?"

Alex hung his head. "I'll explain everything later. Right now, it is important that you believe me when I tell you that he was dead when I entered his office."

"You mean Matteo Conti, don't you?" Lana whispered as all the puzzle pieces fell into place.

"Matteo Conti? Is that the dead man's name?"

"How do you not know his name?" she screamed. "He was the head of Sail

Away Cruises. An hour ago, I was at a party in that same building, helping him celebrate twenty years at the helm."

"Shh!" Alex sprung up and held a finger over her mouth. "I am so sorry. I knew you were in Venice, but I had no idea you would be at the party. How did you get an invitation?"

Alex's tone was so casual, she wondered whether they were living the same reality. "Are you kidding? Why does it matter why I was there? You are the one that needs to answer questions right now, not me."

"Right, okay, what else do you want to know?"

Lana wanted to scream again, but bit her tongue instead. "There were at least twenty security guys guarding the front entrance. How did you get into the building? And why did you go into Matteo's office, instead of one of the other protesters?"

"A few of our members created a distraction by the entrance so the six of us could sneak up the fire escape and get into the top floor of the building. Once we were inside, it was luck of the draw as to who went into which office. I saw that his door was still closed, so I opened it," Alex said glumly. "There was a lamp on, and I could see an older man slumped over his desk at a strange angle. I couldn't see the blood from the doorway. Looking back, I should have asked one of the others to go with me, but I reacted automatically. I had to see if he was alright."

Lana couldn't fault his actions, knowing she would have done the same.

"When I got closer, I could see that he had a nasty head wound that looked fresh and his desk was covered in blood. I checked his pulse anyway, but didn't find one. When I turned to leave and warn the others, the door opened and a cleaning lady switched on the light. When she saw me standing next to the dead guy, she began screaming bloody murder. I had to push her aside to get out. I know I should have stayed and explained, but my hands were red with the man's blood, and it was a gut instinct to run." Alex's voice cracked, and he dropped his head to hide his face.

"If you only checked his pulse, how did you get blood all over you?"

"I had a bag of pig's blood attached to my waist. When I ran off, it got caught on the door handle and burst. It must have splashed onto my pants and shirt, but I didn't notice until I got here."

"But why did you have pig's blood with you in the first place? And how did you get away? I saw on the news that several protesters were arrested after they had rappelled down the building. Is that how you got out?"

Alex's head shot up. "It's on the news?"

"Of course it is! That's why I knew that Matteo had been murdered in his office tonight. However, the news did not mention that my boyfriend was the one that found him."

Before Alex could react, another round of police sirens approaching their street cut their conversation short.

"Did someone see me come inside this hotel?" Alex wondered aloud, slipping down further into his chair.

"You are covered in blood. I wouldn't be surprised if someone did see you and called the police," Lana said as she sprung up to look out the window.

"What do you see?" Alex asked.

"There are about twenty police officers getting out of boats, and they appear to be heading towards our hotel. Oh, Alex—I think they are going to search the rooms! What are we going to do?"

11

Steamy Escape

Shouting in the hallway caused Lana to jump back from the window and race over to the door's peephole. Two uniformed officers were pounding on the door across from her. "Police! Open the door!"

She watched as the officers entered the room and closed the door behind them. Seconds later, they exited and knocked on the next room.

Lana pulled back from the peephole. "They must be searching all of the rooms. You have to get out of here."

She ran back to the balcony, but there were far too many police and bystanders milling about for Alex to climb down unseen. But where could she hide him? She scanned the room, considering the potential hiding places when an idea struck.

"Quick, get into the bathroom!" She shooed Alex into the marble-covered space. Inside was a glass-enclosed shower, free-standing bathtub, and toilet.

She turned the shower water on to hot.

"Do you want me to get undressed, as well?" Alex asked while watching her, alert as a cat.

Lana pulled her hotel's complimentary bathrobe closer around her neck. Considering how quickly the police were moving down the hallway, they must not be spending much time in each room, Lana reckoned. She hoped to use that to her advantage. "No, but when the police knock on the door, I want you to hide in the shower. Let's give it a chance to steam up first."

They both listened as the officers worked their way down the opposite side of the hallway, before they crossed over to Lana's side. When the police knocked on her door, she put her finger to her lips. Only after the police began pounding a third time and shouted that they were using a keycard to enter did Lana dip her head into the spray, getting her hair wet, and turn off the water.

"Give me a second, I'm in the shower," she yelled at the top of her lungs. Lana waved for Alex to enter the enclosed glass space, hoping that the condensation on the glass would hide him well enough. She threw a towel over one side for good measure and then rushed to the door.

The police pushed it open as soon as she released the handle, then sprung back into the hallway when they realized Lana was dressed in only a terrycloth bathrobe and her hair was dripping wet.

"Pardon, *signora*, but we have reason to believe a murder suspect was seen entering this hotel a few minutes ago. We need to search each room."

Lana pulled her bathrobe tighter around her body as her eyes widened. "Oh, no—a murderer, here? Do come inside."

She stepped back, allowing the two officers to enter. One opened the closet and cabinets she had considered hiding Alex in, while the other opened the bathroom door. A cloud of hot steam greeted the second policeman.

"I was in the shower when you knocked and had locked the door. I doubt he's hiding in there," Lana said.

The officer's forehead crinkled. "Why did you lock the door if you are alone?"

"Force of habit, I guess." She grinned sheepishly and shrugged.

The officer leaned his head into the steamy room and gave it a cursory scan.

"All clear," he said to his partner after closing the bathroom door.

"Thank you for your cooperation, *signora*."

"No problem. Good luck, officers," Lana said, as sincerely as she could. After they exited, she fell back against the closed door, trembling from the stress. *So much for a fatality-free trip.*

12

Coast is Clear

When Lana opened the shower door, Alex's woeful expression made her want to wrap her arms around his neck and tell him that everything was going to be okay. But considering she didn't know how he was involved in Matteo's murder, how could she offer such a reassurance?

"How did you think up that shower trick?" Alex whispered.

"I recall seeing something like that in an old spy film," Lana said and sank onto the corner of the bathtub as the rush of adrenaline left her body.

A volley of knocks and angry voices on the other side of her door made both of them freeze.

"Do you think the police are back?" Alex asked, his jaw clenching.

Lana listened carefully, realizing that she recognized the voices. "No, those are my tour guests. You better get back in the shower. I don't want anyone to see you in here, especially in that state," she said, pointing at his clothes.

Part of her wanted to ignore her guests' needs so she and Alex could talk. Instead, she sucked up her breath and reminded herself that she was the senior guide on this trip. She was being paid good money to reassure her guests.

After Alex retreated to the shower, Lana looked through the peephole. Two of her guests were standing in front of her door.

"Lana Hansen, are you in there?" Rhonda cried out.

"Yes, I am," she yelled back. "But I was in the shower when the police

66

knocked. Please give me a minute to get dressed."

She dressed in record time, then opened the door and stepped out into the hallway, to prevent her guests from coming inside.

"We checked the news after the police searched our room and saw that Matteo has been murdered! What in the devil happened at that party after we left?" Rhonda demanded. "And just now, the police burst their way into our room as if we were the criminals! I was still in my dressing gown, for goodness' sake."

"There is a killer on the loose, Rhonda," Carmen said, her voice filled with more excitement than angst. "I can't believe we left the party before it got exciting. Are all Wanderlust tours this invigorating?"

"That's not the word I would use for it," Lana mumbled, realizing that the curse she hoped to escape from had followed her to Venice. Although it wasn't one of her guests that had been murdered, it appeared that her group was at the scene of the crime and, as such, would be investigated by the police.

"Will this ever stop?" she wondered, unintentionally speaking the words aloud.

"I suppose once the police have caught their suspect," Rhonda replied. "But why do the police think his killer is hiding in this hotel?"

"BBC News said something about him being spotted running down the street behind our hotel." Lana looked down the hallway, relieved to see the two officers were walking up to the next floor. "It looks like the police are done with us, at least for tonight. Are you two going to be alright?"

Carmen waved off Lana's question. "We're fine. Rhonda, why don't we head back to our room?"

Rhonda waffled, but did follow her friend back down the hallway. "Alright. Good night, Lana."

After she pulled her door closed and leaned against it, Alex opened the bathroom door slightly and whispered, "Is the coast clear?"

Lana nodded as she blew out her cheeks. "The police just walked upstairs, so we should be alright for tonight. We fooled them once, but I can't hide you in here forever."

Alex's eyes widened, but before he could respond, Lana's phone began to ring.

"What now?" she grumbled.

"Lana, we have a situation." For the first time since she had met him, Lana heard hesitation and uncertainty in Tom's voice. "I am still at the ball. There was a break-in upstairs, and the police are questioning all of the guests. George is pretty mad, and the Windsors want to leave, but the police won't allow them to. I don't know what to do. Do you have any suggestions?"

Here we go again, she sighed. "Unfortunately, I do. I'll be right over. In the meantime, hang tight and tell our guests to answer all of the police's questions as truthfully as they can."

Alex raised his eyebrows.

Lana hung up before explaining, "The police are questioning all of the guests at the party, and my clients are upset. I need to go back and help Tom deal with this. I know this sounds silly, but do you mind hiding out in the bathroom until I get back? If the guests hear the television or see the light on, they might assume that I'm in here and knock. And if I don't answer, they might get suspicious. That Carmen is sharp as a tack—nothing seems to get past her."

"I'll do anything you ask. I just appreciate you letting me hide out here."

Alex's almost formal tone cut through to her soul. She gently took his hands and looked into his eyes. "I may not like what you did, but I still care what happens to you."

When his face brightened and he started to move in for a kiss, Lana released her grip and stepped back. "Please don't push it. I need time to process this, but I don't have that luxury at the moment. I have to get back to my guests."

"I understand. I'll be waiting here, in the bathroom. I love you, Lana Hansen."

"And I you, Alex Wright," she said, as cheerily as she could. Until Alex explained why he had taken part in a radical protest action without telling her, her heart would not feel light.

13

All Hands on Deck

When Lana returned to the party, the festive atmosphere had been replaced by a scene worthy of a television crime drama. A plethora of police boats were tied up to the canal's edge, and seemingly hundreds of officers were milling about the scene, clumped together in small groups searching and questioning anyone that crossed their paths. Their feverish motion reminded Lana of a colony of ants.

She made her way towards the main entrance, assuming correctly that she would be stopped before she could get inside. After she'd shown two policemen her passport and explained her reason for returning, one escorted her upstairs to the main ballroom. The dance floor was now a surreal mix of police uniforms, Carnevale masks, and medieval garb.

After a few minutes of searching, she spotted Tom and her guests gathered together in a loose circle at the back of the expansive hall. She rushed over to them, glad she didn't have to wrestle with her formal ball gown or high-heeled shoes as she maneuvered through the crowds.

As soon as she approached, George began to curse and fuss. "How dare the police hold us here! We had nothing to do with the murder."

Lana nodded, trying her best to remain calm while she assessed the situation. "I know it is frustrating, but they need to speak with everyone present, just in case someone saw or heard something that could be useful to their investigation. Them holding you here does not mean they suspect you of doing anyone harm."

"Good, because we are innocent, obviously. Sure, Matteo and I didn't always see eye to eye, but that doesn't mean I strangled him," George fumed.

"Was he strangled? On the news they said something about him being bludgeoned to death," Lana murmured.

"Stabbed, strangled, bludgeoned—I don't know how he was killed because I did not do it! That just proves that I had nothing to do with the murder, so why are the police still holding me here?" George's voice rose higher and higher until it filled the hall. His question drew the attention of one of the detectives, who sauntered over to their group, his notepad already open and pen at the ready. A second officer, at least ten years his junior, followed him over to their group.

"Good evening, I am Detective Esposito. We are holding you here, because we must interview everyone present before you may leave."

"When can we go back to our hotel? My head is killing me," George stated. When Lana looked at her guest more closely, she noticed that his already puffy face was swollen and red, as if he had either been crying or had overexerted himself.

"I understand your discomfort, yet a man is dead. We are obligated to investigate this crime, don't you think?" the detective asked. His patient tone seemed to defuse George's bluster.

"Sorry, I wasn't thinking. It's been a long night," George apologized, averting his gaze.

"Sir, let me begin with you. After you have answered my questions, you will be free to go."

George brightened up at that prospect. "Certainly. Fire away, inspector."

"Firstly, may I see your passport?"

"Alright." George dug it out of a pocket sewn inside the waistcoat, then handed it to the detective. The senior officer glanced over it, before handing it to the younger officer, who snapped two photos of it with his telephone, before returning it to the inspector.

"Wait a second, is that legal? Aren't you supposed to just jot down our name and the passport number?"

Detective Esposito smiled. "We have to interview more than two hundred guests and staff members tonight. I would rather my officers spend their time interviewing potential witnesses, instead of transcribing all of their contact information. If you don't like our methods, I can take you down to the station after we are done here and type your contact information straight into the computer myself."

George grabbed his passport out of the inspector's hand. "You've already taken the pictures, haven't you? You got what you wanted."

Esposito raised a pen over his notepad. "George Fretwell, where were you when Matteo Conti's body was discovered?"

He pointed to the bar. "I was standing over there. I had just ordered a vodka martini when Matteo's assistant rushed downstairs and began screaming that he was dead. And after that, it was a blur of guests racing out of the hall. It was chaos, so I just stood by the bar and drank my drink."

Detective Esposito's pen froze mid-word. "Wait a moment, one of the hosts makes clear that the man of honor has been murdered, and your reaction is to casually sip your cocktail?"

"What else was I supposed to do—run around like an idiot and pull out my hair? I didn't know the guy that well. Yes, I invested in his business, but we weren't dating. And that girl did not say there was a killer on the loose, only that her boss was dead. I didn't see anyone wielding a knife or anything like that."

"Fair point," the detective replied as he noted George's answer in his little black book. "Are you traveling with your wife?"

"What do you mean?" George asked. "How did you know I was married?"

"The ring on your finger."

"We came over to together, but she went left earlier than I did. She's at the hotel, I think." George said the last sentence so softly that Lana was not certain the officer heard him.

"Do you mean to tell me that you do not know exactly where your wife is?"

"She's a grown woman—she can take care of herself."

"If you arrived together, why did she leave earlier than you? Does it have anything to do with the loud argument that several guests have mentioned? Between you, your wife, and the deceased, if I understood them correctly."

George's face colored red as he stammered, "I was considering investing more money in Sail Away Cruises, but Matteo was pushing me to finance more than I felt comfortable doing. I told him he could take my offer or leave it. We had both had too much to drink, so we might have raised our voices, but it was not an argument."

Lana lowered her head to ensure the policeman did not see her perplexed expression. *Why was he lying?* she thought. Based on their very public fight, it was not the money that was the problem, but Matteo's untoward advances towards George's wife that created the bad blood. Anyone in the hall who spoke English could confirm that.

"And what did he decide?" Esposito asked.

George shrugged. "I don't know, he was killed before we could talk again. I always knew the environmentalists would get him one day."

The detective cocked his head. "What do you mean exactly?"

George stood a bit straightener. "Matteo was always pushing the limits of legality, which is why I am pulling my money out of Sail Away Cruises. The returns are not worth the risk."

Lana's mouth fell open. Up until the party, George had continually sung Matteo's praises, and assured the Windsors that Sail Away Cruises was financially and morally sound.

"Matteo told me he had been testing the waters by approaching different lawmakers and inspectors to see who may be open to bribes. The UNESCO watchdogs were making things quite difficult; however, Matteo said he was making headway and it was only a matter of time before his ships were cruising past Saint Mark's Square again. He wanted to go big and have a new fleet ready to take over the market before the rest wormed their way back in. That's why he needed a large cash injection."

Lana paled, glad the protesters outside had taken the rumors more seriously than she had. They were right; all it would take was for one cruise ship company to regain access to the Venetian Lagoon, and then the rest would be able to follow suit. The protesters' presence out on the streets—

and their continuing political pressure on the city government to ensure the island-city received the protection it desperately needed—was exactly what was required.

However, when Lana realized that if the environmentalists were blamed for Matteo's death, her boyfriend would be suspect number one.

"You can't assume it was the environmentalists that did it," she mumbled. "Matteo did not come across as a nice person. I can imagine he made many enemies, and several of them were here tonight, based on the arguments that I witnessed. He may have been dead before that environmentalist the cleaner saw fleeing even entered the room."

Esposito's eyes narrowed as he turned to get a good look at her. "How did you know about the cleaner, Miss…?"

"I'm Lana Hansen, and I'm leading a tour here. These are my clients," she said and gestured to her group. "I went back to the hotel before the party ended because I was tired, and saw a breaking news report about Matteo's murder before I came back. The presenter said a cleaning woman saw a man fleeing from Matteo's office, and that was why you were organizing a manhunt across the city center."

Lana couldn't recall whether Alex had told her about the cleaner, or whether she had seen it on the television. But she figured the inspector would not be able to watch the news until after she and her guests had gone back to the hotel.

The inspector turned to his subordinate and began cursing in Italian. The young officer listened quietly, growing redder in the cheeks the longer his boss spoke.

"Nothing is a secret in this city," the inspector added in English. "I haven't even finished investigating the scene of the crime, and crucial information about the case is already out on the streets."

"Your men did force their way into our hotel rooms and search them without ever telling us why they were there. It was a bit scary. I was actually glad that the news explained what was going on, because your men certainly did not."

When the inspector spoke again, the bluster had left his voice. "Perhaps we could have communicated better, but my men were trying to find a fleeing suspect. Let us move forward. Why did you return to the party?"

Lana nodded at Tom, standing close by. "When my fellow guide called to say our clients were being questioned by the police, I thought it prudent to return and see if I could be of help."

A rapid clicking of heels, approaching fast, made them all turn. It was Vittoria, Sail Away Cruises' vice president, and she looked angry. "Excuse me, several guests informed me that someone in this group accused Sail Away Cruises of bribing officials. Who is spreading these untruths?"

"They aren't lies—that's what Matteo told me," George replied.

Vittoria threw her hands onto her hips, her mask flipping around her wrist as she did. "That is not true. Please don't use this investigation to repeat baseless rumors. Sail Away is going to have a hard enough time recovering from this blow, as it is. Even if Matteo had wanted to, there is no point in bribing anyone because it is simply not possible to circumvent the new regulations."

She spoke so loudly that everyone in the room could easily hear her, which Lana assumed was intentional. When she turned to George, her tone softened slightly. "Matteo was apparently telling you what he thought you wanted to hear, in order to get you to invest more. To be honest, I do wonder if Matteo had not spread those rumors himself, so that the environmental groups would protest tonight. Their presence would guarantee that his party would make the front page of every newspaper in Italy. He truly believed any publicity was better than none."

Matteo got his wish, though not in the way that he had hoped, Lana thought.

"And you are?" Detective Esposito asked.

"Vittoria Russo, acting CEO of Sail Away Cruises."

That went fast, Lana thought. What a rollercoaster ride Vittoria had been on tonight. She began the evening thinking Matteo would announce her as his successor, then she had to deal with losing out on her expected promotion in a very public way, yet before the night was through, she ended up taking Matteo's place, after all.

"When did you last see Matteo?"

"I was walking upstairs to retrieve a contract for a new client who was attending the party when I heard the cleaning lady screaming. Then Bianca began yelling about Matteo being dead. When we crossed paths on the staircase, I was almost at the landing, so I went up anyway. When I opened the door to the floor, I saw three people dressed in black running along the corridor. I panicked and ran back downstairs."

"Those were members of the Earth Warriors. Several of them rappelled out of your office windows to reach the back garden. I am afraid they broke one of them and knocked over a cabinet."

"Great, yet another mess to clean up."

The inspector turned his attention to the Windsors. "What is your relationship to the deceased?"

"Kathy and I own Windsor Custom Watercraft. Our company built a fleet of ocean-going vessels for Sail Away Cruises, and we were here in Venice to decide on a delivery date."

"Several witnesses mentioned an argument between you and the deceased. What was it about?" The inspector's tone was so casual, it belied the seriousness of the words he spoke.

The couple looked at one another before Kathy spoke. "When we saw Matteo at the party, he was surprised to see us, which makes no sense!"

"He told us that we had been uninvited," Dave interjected in a calmer tone. "Who does that? This was our first European contract, and we were so excited about completing it, we even paid for our two builders to join us." He gestured to Harry and Joe. "But Matteo couldn't be bothered to call and tell us himself, so he asked his assistant to uninvite us. But apparently she didn't have to the guts to follow through. So here we are."

"That's not entirely true," Vittoria said. "Matteo did tell Bianca to cancel their invitations because he wanted to work with another company, but I wanted you two here. Matteo was supposed to be announcing his retirement tonight, meaning the future of the company would have been in my hands. I want to continue working with Windsor Custom Watercraft, even if Matteo did not."

Dave and Kathy lit up as relief washed over their faces.

"After this is all over, can we talk?" Vittoria asked. "Preferably before you leave Venice."

"Yes!" Kathy squealed.

"We would love to meet with you and discuss our future together," Dave added.

"Vittoria?" a soft voice asked. Lana looked towards the source, spotting Bianca standing just behind the acting CEO. "The board of directors wants to speak to you when you are done here."

"Certainly, thanks for letting me know, Bianca," she said, before waving in their direction.

"Are we done here?" Vittoria asked the detective.

Esposito smiled, baring his teeth. It wasn't a friendly gesture. "Please don't leave the party until my men have a copy of your contact information."

She chuckled. "Don't worry, I'll be here all night, by the looks of things."

When Bianca also began to walk away, the inspector stopped her. "Are you Bianca de Luca, Matteo's assistant?"

"Yes," she said. Her startled expression reminded Lana of a deer trapped in headlights. *No*, she thought as she studied Bianca's small frame and round cheeks, *more like a mouse about to eaten by a cat.*

"I have several witnesses mentioning a museum representative and Matteo arguing over a statue of a gondola. But we have not found it up in his office. Where was it taken after Matteo's speech?"

Bianca looked to Vittoria, now chatting animatedly with several older men, presumably the board of directors. "Vittoria took it up to his office after his speech. She was supposed to put it in the safe. Do you need me to open it for you?"

"No, the door to the safe was open when we arrived, and there was nothing inside but paperwork. Was it unusual for him to have the statue here at the office?"

Bianca nodded. "He only brought it in once a year, to show off during this party. The rest of the time, he kept it at his home. I believe he displays it in his living room, but I have never been to his house so I can't be certain."

"Did you know before the party started that he was not planning on giving it to the museum tonight?"

Bianca shook her head. "No, but Matteo must have changed his mind on a whim, again. He was an egotistical man who loved to play with people's lives, as if they have no significance. But we all have feelings and needs, too."

Lana couldn't help but notice how the assistant's language switched from general to personal, quite rapidly. Considering Matteo had essentially fired her earlier this evening, she could imagine the young lady was rather upset. What would Matteo's death mean for her? Would Vittoria keep her on, or would she promote her own personal assistant? The acting CEO had also been rather critical of Bianca's abilities earlier, which probably meant that she would soon be out of a job.

"Alright, thank you. You can go now," Detective Esposito said to Bianca before returning his attention to Dave and Kathy.

"And where were you when Matteo's body was discovered?" the inspector asked.

"We were all standing by the bar, having one last round, when we heard the screaming. The staircase and elevators are on the other side of the hall—there was no way any of us could have had anything to do with his murder."

"Did anyone see you?" the inspector asked.

Harry laughed. "Yeah, everyone around us, but we didn't know anyone here, except the other tour guests and a few of the Sail Away staff."

The inspector glanced over his notebook before closing it with a snap. "Thank you for your time. If you will excuse me, I have many more interviews to conduct tonight." He clicked his heels and bowed slightly before adding, "Enjoy your time in Venice."

Lana and the rest murmured "good night" then turned towards the coat check.

"I cannot wait to crawl into bed," Kathy said as she took Dave's hand.

"Me, either," Lana replied. Only after she followed her group out the door did she remember that she was not yet done for the night. Alex was still hiding in her bathroom. At least, if he hadn't been discovered by now.

14

True Colors

Lana felt like James Bond when she tapped lightly on the door twice, paused for two seconds, then knocked three more times before entering. The irregular pattern of knocks was meant to let her boyfriend know it was her, and not a snooping guest, a hotel employee, or the police.

No, my life is not cool enough to be Bond worthy. More like Inspector Clouseau, she thought as she opened the door.

Alex, true to his word, did not come out of the bathroom, but waited for her to join him. She opened the door softly, smiling at him as she entered. Concerned someone might hear them talking and ask her about it, they had already agreed to only converse inside the bathroom with the door closed.

"You were gone so long. Are you alright?" He rose to greet her, presenting Lana with her first conundrum. As much as she loved Alex and trusted that they would get through this current crisis, his lies hurt her deeply, and she wanted time to get her head straight before they went back to pretending like everything was hunky dory.

"I'm okay, thanks," she said, averting her face so his kiss connected with her cheek instead of her lips.

Alex sighed as he sat back down on the closed toilet lid. Lana perched on the edge of the tub, turning so their legs didn't accidentally touch.

"What happened? Did the police say anything about me or the other protesters?"

"The police didn't tell us anything that was not already reported on in the news. But there were hundreds of guests to interview, so I bet it will take them a while to process all of the information they gather tonight."

Alex nodded, his expression glum.

"Let's put the protest action aside for a moment. What can you tell me about the dead man and his office?" Lana asked, hoping he had seen something that might point them to the real murderer.

"Honestly, I was so focused on the victim, I don't really recall anything else in his office."

Lana blew out her cheeks. "Okay, what can you tell me about the position of his body or the wound?"

"There was still a little blood coming out of his head wound. He had been struck here." Alex pointed to his forehead, above his left eye. "And the wound was quite large, but only part of it seemed deep. I know it sounds strange, but that's what I noticed. I had just put my fingers on his neck to feel for a pulse when the door opened and that cleaning lady began to scream."

Alex hung his head. "I wish I had been paying more attention to my surroundings, but as soon as that woman started yelling for help, I ran out of there as fast as I could."

"How did you get away without the security guards catching you?" Lana whispered, her mind still trying to process all that her boyfriend was telling her.

"Our leader had set up several cables so we could rappel down once we had completed our tasks. We had transportation waiting for us, as well. We figured we could slide down while security was climbing up the stairs. That part worked as planned, but two of our team were captured before they could get into the boat."

"Your leader? Did you join a cult and not tell me?"

He started to laugh, but one look at her face and he grew still.

"Alex, there is nothing funny about this situation. Why were you participating in the protest action? You aren't an environmental activist, and you certainly don't live in Venice. Or is there something else you aren't telling me?" Lana folded her arms over her torso.

Alex looked away.

"You owe me some answers, mister! What exactly were you planning on doing at Sail Away Cruises?"

The anxiety in her tone apparently prompted him to respond. "We were supposed to go into each office, grab any paperwork we could find, and pour the pig's blood over the computers, before meeting back at our exit point. Once we were finished with the offices, we were going to hang a banner out of the top-floor windows. There were six of us, and we spread out as soon as we were inside, so as to get the most done in the shortest amount of time as possible."

Lana shook her head as she studied her boyfriend's face. Who was this person before her? His words didn't mesh with the Alex she knew and loved.

"We were trying to send a message, not hurt anyone!" he cried.

"How do you even know the other members of the group?"

"Do you remember me working a weeklong conference in Zurich a few months ago?"

Lana nodded. "Yes, you were in Switzerland while I was in Paris."

"It was a conference for organizations working to save the environment. All of the bigger charities and watchdogs had stands there, as well as several protest organizations. At one of the networking sessions, I got to talking to a man who I thought worked for the World Wildlife Fund. We hit it off and ended up having dinner a few times together."

"Okay, I guess that's not weird."

"It is unusual, but it was a small conference. We kept running into each other, and he was easy to talk to."

"Alright, please continue," Lana urged.

"On the last night of the conference, the guy asked if I wanted to join him for a boat ride the next day. He made a show of winking at me as he said it, but at the time, I figured he had something in his eye. I said, sure, and didn't think any more about it. When I showed up the next morning, he was dressed in all black and was surprised that I wasn't, as well. That's when he told me that the boat ride was a protest action to block fishermen who had already exceeded their quota from leaving the wharf."

"Wait—what? Why didn't he tell you earlier what he was really doing?"

"He thought I knew he was with Earth Warriors and assumed I would know he meant the boat ride was one of their actions."

"So what did you do?" Lana asked, feeling her nervousness growing by the second. Alex was not a wimp by any means, but he also was not the kind of person who would willingly take part in a radical protest action.

"I changed into my darkest clothes and joined him."

She stared at her boyfriend for a moment, then held out her hand. "Hello, I'm Lana Hansen. I don't think we've met."

His face caved in. "It's not like that. I'm the same Alex."

"No, you are an environmental warrior and have been for months!"

"It wasn't a violent protest. All we did is block their way for a few hours; we didn't torpedo them or sink their ship. And besides, the guy is completely normal—not some crazy, long-haired hippie. He's just really passionate about nature."

"What's his name?"

"River," Alex mumbled.

"Figures." Lana sprung up and began to pace the room. "Zurich was four months ago. When were you planning on telling me about this new side of yourself?"

"Lana, I went along on that boat ride expecting to be bored, but I had the time of my life. It was so exhilarating, being part of something bigger. You know I love to rock climb, but this was even more of an adrenaline kick. I had to do it again. Their protests aren't violent, or at least they aren't supposed to be, and they do force companies and governments to change their behavior."

"How many of these Earth Warrior protests have you taken part in?"

Alex shifted uncomfortably in his chair. "A few, but only on the periphery. I'm not a card-carrying member. Their actions take a lot of behind-the-scenes organization, and that is one of my specialties."

Lana bit her lip to try to stifle the stream of tears building up behind her eyes. How could he have lied to her, and for so long?

Alex gently took her hand and held it, gazing at her with puppy-dog eyes.

"Lana, I can see what you are thinking, but I am not Ron. I did not sleep with anyone or do anything else to compromise our relationship. I guess I was discovering a new side of myself, one I didn't know existed until a couple months ago. I'm still the Alex you know and love."

"Except for the fact that you lied about where you were and who you were with multiple times. You know I have some serious trust issues thanks to my ex," Lana spat back, her anger boiling to the surface. Her first—and now former—husband, Ron, had been fooling around with his assistant for months before he finally admitted to the affair, via text message, no less. In all that time, Lana had not the slightest clue that he had been cheating on her.

"I can't decide what is worse—that you have been lying to me for months or the fact that I didn't suspect a thing."

"I was trying to protect you!"

"Then why didn't you trust me enough to tell me the truth?"

"Because I didn't want you to worry, but I didn't want you to try to talk me out of taking part in them, either," he spat, his face paling as soon as the words were out.

Finally, we get to the core of the matter, Lana thought.

"Oh, Lana, I didn't mean it that way. I do enjoy taking part in the actions because they serve a higher purpose. It's not just the adrenaline kick, but that is a big part of it."

Alex ran a hand through his wavy red hair. "I've worked so many conferences this past year that they are all running together. You get to see Europe's most incredible cities and monuments, but all I see are the insides of trade show and conference centers. When River asked me to change clothes and join him on that boat, I said yes because I was craving a little adventure in my life, too."

He took her hands, pleading with his eyes for forgiveness. "I am so ashamed. I never wanted to lie to you, but it's become a passion. Sail Away Cruises was bribing everyone they could, in an attempt to get their ships back into Venice's lagoon. That is why we were targeting them."

"'We,'" Lana echoed. Alex clearly felt like he was part of the group. "For someone who claims to be on the periphery, you sure seem to be right in the middle of this one."

"I wasn't supposed to be. When I showed up, River told me one of their protesters had been arrested that morning and couldn't take part. When he asked me to take their place, I didn't realize it was going to be so intense, until it was too late to back out."

"Alright, but you still have not explained why you didn't think I would understand why you wanted to take part in these actions."

Alex leaned back and studied her face for a long minute, before finally answering. "Remember that documentary we watched about Greenpeace and their Aurora Bridge protest?"

"You mean those fools who hung off the bridge on teeny-tiny ropes for days on end? That was so reckless, they could have died," Lana retorted.

"See what I mean?" Alex smiled sadly. "You were completely freaked out for them, and perhaps rightfully so. But they were trying to stop two trawlers known for overfishing from leaving Lake Union. Their actions brought international media attention to an issue that is too often overlooked by the press."

Lana breathed in deeply through her nose. "What does the Aurora Bridge protest have to do with you being hunted by the Venetian police?"

"River organized a similar action in England a few weeks ago. That's the kind of protest that I have been taking part in. When you reacted so strongly to that documentary, I lost the nerve to tell you."

"So it's my fault you lied to me?" Lana asked.

Alex's face fell.

She stood before him. "I think I understand what kind of person River is. Now I have to figure out who you are, Alex Wright. You say that you lied to me, in order to save my feelings from getting hurt. But the lying is the worst part. That's not okay, under any circumstances."

When she locked her eyes onto his, Alex had trouble holding her gaze. "You have to be honest with me—have you taken part in any protest, other than the one in Zurich and tonight's break-in?"

"I swear to you that I did not. I should have told you about Zurich right away, but I didn't want you to be concerned for me. Now I know that you worrying would have been better than this. I didn't mean to keep anything from you."

When he leaned in to kiss her, Lana jerked away. "I'm sorry, but it's too soon. Can you give me time to process this?"

Alex grabbed her shoulders, gently yet firmly. "If that is what you need, then I'll back down. But know this—I didn't mean to become an environmentalist, it just kind of happened. But not telling you was the stupidest decision I have ever made, especially if it means I might lose you."

When Lana refused to meet his gaze, he threw up his hands. "I can tell we aren't going to resolve this tonight, but I can't go back out onto the streets looking like this. My wallet and passport are in my suitcase, which I left at the apartment the environmentalists rented in town."

"Let me guess—your rendezvous point?" Lana quipped, causing Alex's face to darken.

"If you could help me get a T-shirt and a pair of jeans in the morning, I can go over to the apartment tomorrow and get my passport back."

Lana looked at her boyfriend, wondering whether she knew him at all. "And here I felt like James Bond when I knocked to enter the room. You really are living the life, aren't you?"

Alex ignored her gibe. "The cleaner got a good look at me, but I was out of the dead man's office before the security guards arrived. According to the news reports, the police haven't identified me yet. If I can get out of the country tomorrow, I should be able to get back to Seattle without trouble."

Lana nodded, feeling numb. "Alright. I can pick up some clothes for you in the gift shop before my first tour starts. We are heading over to Murano in the morning and will be there all day."

Alex gazed down at her. "I promise to leave as soon as I am properly clothed. Can I please sleep on the couch tonight?"

15

Full Speed Ahead

April 23—Day Five of the Wanderlust Tour in Venice, Italy

Lana awoke to the sound of Italian. "No!" she whimpered and shot up in bed, momentarily convinced it was the police arresting Alex. Only after she oriented herself did she notice that she was alone and the television was on.

Alex popped his head out of the bathroom and a wave of steam floated out. "Good morning, sunshine. I haven't seen my face on TV yet. I guess that's a good thing."

His attempt at a joke didn't elicit a smile from her.

When he walked towards her with only a small towel wrapped around his waist, it took all of Lana's willpower to ignore his tight abs and strong arms and keep her eyes locked on his.

"I'm sorry about leaving the television on. I couldn't sleep and wanted to see if there was any new information about the murder. When I didn't see any, I decided to take a shower. I didn't mean to wake you."

"It's alright." Lana stretched her arms over her head and yawned. Her sleep had been fitful and full of nightmares, most of them involving Alex being arrested or worse. When she did drift off, the sun was just starting to rise over the canal. As much as she wanted to call in sick today so she could deal with this personal situation, she knew she could not. Not only would it be incredibly unprofessional, today was a busy day and Tom was not yet ready to deal with herding the group to their many stops on his own.

Lana glanced at the clock, realizing she had to be downstairs in the breakfast room within the hour, where she would be expected to cheerily help her group before they left for a full day of activities.

Instead of brooding on Alex's betrayal, she forced herself to focus on helping him get out of Italy. She would have three more days in Venice to contemplate the future of their relationship before she could fly back to Seattle and talk it out, face to face.

"Have the police made any progress on finding the real killer?"

Alex shook his head, his expression grim. "It does not look like it. If the news media are to be believed, the police are only interested in finding me right now." He grabbed the remote control lying on the couch next to him and flipped from the local Italian news station to BBC World News. "I even made the world news, though luckily my face is not visible."

Lana's stomach sunk as she took in the grainy video of several protesters rappelling down the side of Sail Away Cruises headquarters. Splashed across the bottom of the screen was a red banner with the text "Manhunt in Venice."

"Have they been able to identify you?" she asked, her eyes glued to the images.

"They have several eyewitnesses that saw us rappel down the building so they know the Earth Warriors are involved. But I'm not really part of the group, so my photo is not on their website. And I've never been arrested, so the police can't match my DNA to anything, assuming they did find some at the scene."

"That's a relief," Lana said, feeling a layer of anxiety lifting. "The gift shop should be open in a few minutes. Let me jump in the shower, then I'll go down and get you some clothes."

"Thanks, hon." When he bent over to kiss her, Lana pulled away, making them both blush in embarrassment.

She showered and dressed in record time. The gift shop clerk didn't seem fazed in the slightest that she was purchasing men's clothes and even added in a sample of cologne to her bag.

Once she was back on her floor, Lana checked that none of her clients were in the hallway before she opened her door.

She couldn't remember the last time that Alex looked so grateful as he did when she presented him with his new duds. He dressed quickly and silently, as if he was mentally preparing for the upcoming journey. From what he had told her, the address in question was a short *vaporetto* ride away. If everything went according to plan, he would have his passport and be traveling to the airport before she got her tour group to their water taxi.

"Will you call after you land and let me know that you are home safe?"

Alex pulled her close. "Of course. Lana, I love you with all of my heart, and I cannot express how bad I feel about lying to you. I'll do anything you ask, as long as you promise not to give up on me just yet."

Lana smiled despite her anger and worry, allowing herself to relax into his arms, if only for a moment. She had never met anyone as perfect for her as Alex—at least, so she had thought. Now she had to figure out whether this new version still meshed with the one she knew so well.

"Please be careful," she whispered as he walked to the door. Despite her hurt feelings, Lana couldn't let him go without giving him a kiss. When their lips met, Alex's eyes teared up and he pulled her tight, squeezing so hard she was breathless.

When he released her, Alex looked her deep in the eyes. "I'll call you as soon as I land at SeaTac."

Lana nodded, unable to control her emotions or voice.

Alex squeezed her hand, opened the door, and then he was gone.

Lana closed it softly behind him. Confused and flustered, she stepped out onto the balcony to get one more glimpse of him. Postal boats and garbage collectors cruised up the canal, causing the creamy water to churn in their wake. The facades of the finely decorated palazzos rising up on both sides of the water were lit up in the morning sun. She finally spotted Alex walking along the water's edge, moments before he was swallowed up by the masses of tourists walking the same path.

She stared ahead unseeingly, trying to get her emotions under control. How could her mild-mannered boyfriend be an environmental activist? He didn't seem the type to get worked up enough about anything to actually take part in a protest against it. But apparently there was another side to her boyfriend, a more adventurous one that she could never have guessed existed. So what else was Alex capable of?

What troubled her most was how she had not noticed. Sure, because of their work schedules, they didn't spend every waking moment together. But they did talk or message each other daily and spent as many weekends together as possible. For the past four months, he had apparently lied to her repeatedly about what he was doing. It felt like her ex-husband's betrayal all over again. How could Alex have kept such a big secret to himself? And why didn't he trust her enough to tell her the truth?

Yet, in spite of her hurt feelings, Lana did not want to see him arrested for a crime he didn't commit.

She looked again to the beauty surrounding her, but it didn't offer her the peace of mind that she desired. Knowing there was little else she could do to help Alex, Lana went back inside to get ready. Her guests were counting on her to make their day perfect. And that was exactly what she was going to do.

16

Guest Switcharoo

If Lana thought leading the tour would get her mind off of her boyfriend's troubles, then she was sorely mistaken. When she arrived downstairs, their breakfast table was covered with newspapers in English and Italian, all plastered with images of Matteo and the event venue.

A few of her guests nodded at her arrival, but the rest were nose-deep in the newspapers and didn't seem to notice. Lana grabbed the nearest one and scanned the front-page article. To her relief, the police had not yet identified the man seen running from Matteo's office.

George lowered his paper, snapping it as he did. "It looks like the activist who did Matteo in was part of the same group that was protesting outside the entrance."

"Oh, yeah? This article says it was another group that climbed up the fire escape to get in. Maybe they used the Earth Warriors' protest as a cover for their break-in, to confuse the police?" Carmen suggested.

"Wouldn't the security guards have noticed them climbing up it?" Rhonda asked. "They were swarming all over the place the night of the party."

Dave pointed to an article on page three of the newspaper in his hand. "One of them set off a smoke bomb close to the entrance, and when the rest ran to assist, a small group of protesters snuck upstairs."

"Sneaky indeed," Kathy said. "They must be guilty. I mean, why else did they go to all that trouble to get up to Matteo's office, if they were not planning on harming him?"

Lana prayed that Alex would get his passport and himself out of the country before the police figured out who he was. If the detective had the same thoughts as her guests, her boyfriend would be going to jail for a very long time.

"That's not really the Earth Warriors' *modus operandi*," Carmen replied. "They are known for their radical, yet nonviolent, protests."

"Maybe Matteo interrupted them and things got out of hand. Just because he is dead doesn't mean they meant to kill him when they broke in," Harry offered.

"I wasn't up there, so I wouldn't know," George said.

"Us, either," Kathy hastened to say. "But it is fun to speculate as to who did it."

Yeah, it's fun, alright, Lana thought sarcastically.

"I just read that Matteo was embroiled in several lawsuits," Kathy said.

George's hand shot over and grabbed Kathy's arm. "Do you mean Sail Away Cruises, or Matteo personally?"

"Matteo, not the company," she answered, looking slightly panicked by George's strong reaction.

"Thank goodness." George leaned back in his chair and sighed in relief, before adding, "My money is on those protesters. They were at the right place and had a noble motive. Matteo was a scoundrel and would have done anything to get his boats back into Venice's lagoon."

Lana was again surprised by the fierceness of George's negativity towards Matteo. Because the CEO died under mysterious circumstances, his murder was probably going to affect Sail Away's stock. She would have expected him to show more sorrow about his passing, if only for financial reasons.

"Would you look at that—Matteo's gondola statue is estimated to be worth between twenty and thirty thousand dollars. You were right on the money, Rhonda," Carmen said, pride in her voice as she showed her friend the article and photograph.

"Let me take a look at that." Lana leaned over to get a better look at the photograph, thankful that Carmen had given them a reason to change the subject.

"Huh, it says here that the silversmith was rather famous in his day. That might explain why the museum was initially interested in it. Although the jewels Matteo had added certainly increased its value. Listen to this, Rhonda: 'The sapphires and emeralds around the base represent water, and the pearls are supposed to be waves splashing up against the boat.'"

"I saw it at the party. I still think it is one of the ugliest, most ostentatious things I have ever seen," Kathy chimed in.

Dave leaned over to get a look at the picture before nodding. "I'm with you, hon. Liberace would have loved it."

"It may not be your taste, but it is worth a fortune," Rhonda said. "And now that Matteo is dead, the museum is the official owner. If the police find it, anyway. I bet Matteo's murder will only add to its value—at least, if their marketing department is any good."

"Huh, I've found two mentions of that statue being stolen in the articles I've read so far, but there is no mention of the police having a solid lead as to its whereabouts," Carmen said. "Has anyone else seen a reference to the gondola's theft in their newspapers?"

When the rest shook their heads, she added, "I am surprised it hasn't received more coverage."

George waved away Carmen's remark. "Who cares about some boat statue. Most of Chrissy's necklaces cost more than that gawdy thing. What intrigues me is that the murderer was just two floors above us and we didn't even notice. That's quite a unique experience—being so close to a killer."

"Not for me," Lana muttered, wishing it wasn't so. She had been so certain that her luck would change once Randy retired, and that her tours would no longer involve police interrogations. But fate was not on her side—at least not in the way she had expected.

"What I want to know is why that environmentalist killed him," George continued.

"Maybe the guy was a radical and thought Matteo was some sort of evil seed that had to be reckoned with," Rhonda offered.

"I'll put my money on the museum representative. He was so angry after

Matteo announced he was not yet donating the gondola statue to his museum. And he was so rude outside when we were waiting for a taxi. Remember, Rhonda?" Carmen said, eliciting a nod from her friend.

"It could have been. If the environmentalists didn't get him, there were plenty of other candidates downstairs at the party. Matteo wasn't the easiest guy to work with. Some might say he had it coming—that man lied to or swindled anyone he could. His squabbles with the museum guy and the Windsors attest to that," George said.

"And despite Vittoria's assertions last night after the party, the rumors about Matteo bribing officials may be true," he continued. "I wouldn't be surprised if that's what the lawsuits are all about. Now that he is gone, Vittoria will do everything in her power to distance Sail Away from any nefarious practices or scandal that Matteo created. She is, after all, the acting CEO now."

George's bitter remarks about the murder victim made Lana again wonder what had happened between Matteo and Chrissy in Seattle two years ago. Did they ever have an affair, or was Matteo testing her waters last night, in the hope that she would be receptive to his advances? Suddenly, Lana realized that they were a guest short.

"George, where is Chrissy?"

His expression darkened. "She's not interested in glass."

"Are you certain?" Lana asked, as politely as she could. Chrissy had repeatedly mentioned how much she was looking forward to seeing Murano and buying glass vases directly from the factory showrooms. "The taxi will be here shortly. Should I call up to the room, in case she's changed her mind?"

George's lips pursed. "Don't bother—she's not there. My money is on the hotel spa or salon. She does love to tart herself up."

Before Lana could push George further, a man dressed in sunglasses and a floppy hat burst into the breakfast hall and glanced around frantically. Lana's eyes widened as she realized that the stranger was, in fact, her boyfriend.

Not wanting her guests to notice his presence, Lana sprung up, pushing aside her knife and fork as she did.

"These look dirty. I'm going to grab a clean set. Does anyone need anything else?" she asked, already moving towards the entrance to the breakfast hall, where a table with silverware and napkins was set up.

Her guests were apparently so captivated by the news that they didn't seem to notice her question. Lana skipped over towards the door, close to where her boyfriend was standing.

When she bent her head over the silverware, she snuck a peek at Alex, who was doing his best not to look directly at her.

"Why are you here?" she whispered, keeping her eyes on the utensils in her hand.

Alex sighed as he moved closer and grabbed a fork. "So much for my disguise."

She studied his outfit critically. His new hat and oversized sunglasses looked ridiculous on him, but they did help disguise that gorgeous face of his. "I can still tell who you are, but I know you more intimately than the Venetian police. It should at least prevent them from recognizing you instantly."

When his face brightened, she asked, "Why aren't you at the airport?"

"The police arrested two of the protesters that were up on the top floor with me. One of which is a younger fellow that River already had his doubts about. Apparently he cracked under pressure and told the police about the apartment River had rented. The cops took everything—including my suitcase with my wallet and passport inside. That means I can't get out of the country, and that the police probably now know which name to put to my face."

"Oh, Alex. What are we going to do with you?" Lana pinched her finger, trying in vain to keep the tears from welling up in her eyes.

He hung his head low. "I don't know."

Lana closed her eyes, trying to figure out what their next step would be. "You need to turn yourself in to the police before they find you. But we really need to get you a lawyer first."

"How are we going to do that? I don't speak Italian. And asking someone if they can recommend a good criminal lawyer is not really a great conversation starter."

"You're right about that. But I have a secret weapon, and her name is Dotty

Thompson." Lana looked back to her group; they were still concentrating on the newspapers.

"Give me a minute to talk to the new guide, Tom, and then I'll meet you up at my hotel room. Okay?" She dared not look him directly in the eye, instead catching a glimpse of his slight nod out of the corner of her eye.

Lana grabbed a handful of silverware and turned on her heel, hoping her guests had not been watching them.

She went over to Tom, busy putting a selection of tiny breads into a basket for Carmen and Rhonda, and leaned in close so that the other guests would not hear her. "I know this is bad timing, but I need to check on something with Dotty. Would you mind watching over the group? It shouldn't take more than ten minutes, assuming I can rouse her out of her sleep."

"Sure, I'm happy to help. Is there anything wrong?"

"I'm not certain, to be honest. Dotty sent a strange message about a friend of mine being ill. It might just be a phishing message—it does contain a link to send money—but I'm going to be a nervous wreck until I know that Willow is alright."

Tom laid a hand on Lana's shoulder. "Don't you worry about a thing. I'll think up a reason to delay our departure, if need be."

Lana was afraid he was going to pinch her cheeks. His sincerity came across as patronizing, but right now she was grateful that he was willing to take the reins.

A pit began forming in her stomach as she thought of her upcoming conversation. Thanks to her many connections, her boss was certain to know a good lawyer in Italy.

The only problem was, Lana would first have to explain why Alex needed one.

17

S.O.S.

Lana rushed up to her room, glad to see that Alex was already loitering in front of her door. She shooed him inside and quickly closed it behind them.

"Can I hide out in your hotel room until we figure out what to do next?"

Seeing him in such distress tore at her soul, but she needed to remain firm with him. "How would that work exactly? We are going to be out on different excursions for most of the day. At some point the cleaners are going to want to come inside; I can't leave the 'do not disturb' sign on the door all day without it seeming suspicious."

Lana could feel herself getting more keyed up by the second. She pinched her nose, forcing herself to stop talking and take a lungful of air. Alex's pained and sheepish expression only made her feel worse. As much as she wanted to wrap him up in her arms, she was too worked up about everything that he had done—and the problems it had created—to do so.

The breath of fresh air brought with it a new thought. "I may have a better idea. But I need to ask Dotty's permission first."

Her hands trembled as she waited for her boss to pick up. It was early in the morning in Seattle, but Dotty usually left her phone on, in case of emergencies.

"Hello, Lana. How is Venice treating you?" Dotty sounded so upbeat and chipper.

Lana sighed, hating being the bearer of bad news, yet again. "Venice is amazing. Thanks again for letting me lead this tour. Say, what are you doing up so early?"

"Earl surprised me this morning," Dotty giggled. "He roused me out of bed when it was still dark and convinced me to bike over to Gas Works Park with him. I'm so glad I did what he asked instead of rolling over and ignoring him. We had a mimosa brunch on a picnic blanket as the sun rose over the Seattle skyline. Lana, he prepared it all himself. He really is the most romantic man I have ever met."

"I am so happy for you, Dotty. He sounds like a wonderful guy. I hope we can have dinner together next time I am back in Seattle."

"That sounds great. Earl is going to love you and Alex."

The mention of her boyfriend's name made her choke up.

"So, what's going on, Lana? You usually don't call me so early, unless there is an emergency."

"You got me there," she mumbled, frustrated that her boss saw right through her.

"What happened?"

"Oh, Dotty. Matteo Conti, the CEO of Sail Away Cruises, was murdered last night at that masquerade ball we were invited to. Our whole tour group was there."

"No—not again!"

"And the police think Alex did it. But he ran away before they could arrest him."

Dotty's gasp was audible through the phone line. "As in Alex Wright, your boyfriend and Randy's brother?"

"One and the same."

"But how is he involved?" Dotty stammered. "I thought you said he was working in Berlin this week."

Lana bit her lip to hold back the tears. "I thought he was, too. It's a long story, but the short of it is, he was participating in a protest action organized by Earth Warriors…"

"I know that group," Dotty interjected. "They like to throw paint onto buildings and hang off of bridges."

"Among other things. Alex was taking part in one of their protest actions at the Sail Away offices, on the upper floors during the party, and he is the one who found Matteo's body. But before he could call for help, a cleaning lady found them and began screaming about how Alex had killed Matteo. Which is why he panicked and fled the scene."

"Oh, Lana, this is bad on so many levels."

"No kidding. I think Alex is going to need a lawyer, as soon as humanly possible."

"I don't think so—I know he will," Dotty exclaimed. "I can find him one, but it may take a few hours to do so. It might be better for him to turn himself in now."

"But—"

"No good is going to come by waiting longer. The longer Alex waits, the less inclined the police will be to believe him. Especially since he was spotted fleeing the crime scene."

"I hear what you are saying, but I really think he should wait to turn himself in until he has a lawyer at his side. So far as we know, the police have not yet identified him. And Alex is certain the police won't believe him when he says that Matteo was already dead, unless he has legal representation."

"Alright, as soon as I have a name, I'll give you a call. Are you going to be able to handle leading the rest of the tour with this Alex business going on? I could send Randy over to help," Dotty added, albeit half-heartedly. "He is working in the office this month, but it's not so busy that I can't do without him for a few days."

Lana's stomach sank at the mention of his name. "As much as I love Randy, having him here would make things infinitely worse. Alex is his big brother— once he hears about what is going on, he is going to be far too emotional to be of help."

"You do have a point there."

"Once we get a lawyer, we'll call Randy so Alex can explain what's happened. It will be better coming from him, I suspect."

Dotty breathed a sigh of relief. "Thanks for taking care of that. I did dread having to tell him the bad news."

"I do appreciate your concern, but you can count on me, Dotty. The tour is already halfway over and I have a new guide to train. I can't just leave our clients in the lurch, even for Alex. Besides, there is not much more I can do to help him. Leading the tour will be a great distraction and will keep me in Venice, in case Alex needs me."

"Lana," Dotty said tentatively, as if she was afraid to ask, "when did Alex become one of those Earth Warriors? I don't recall you mentioning it."

Lana laughed bitterly. "Because I didn't know, until he showed up at the hotel covered in blood."

"Oh, child."

"Alex has been lying to me for months about what he has been doing, Dotty. And I'm not sure how to deal with it yet."

"Don't make any rash decisions right now—you will regret it if you do. You have been under a lot of stress these past few months. I can imagine you don't have the mental space to deal with Alex's current predicament on top of everything else. Why don't you take a week off after this tour? Maybe you and Alex can get away and talk things out. If Tom is as good as you say, then he can take your place."

"As long as we can ensure Alex doesn't end up in police custody, that sounds like a great idea."

She knew her boyfriend was a good person and understood his reasons for not telling her—whether she agreed with them or not. He hadn't slept with another woman or done anything to dishonor their relationship. But he had kept a side of himself hidden from her, and for several months. Did he truly believe that she would not have tried to accept his choice to participate in the protest actions? Or was keeping it a secret from her part of the thrill?

Lana paused and gathered up the nerve to ask her boss one more favor. "I just haven't figured out what to do with Alex while we are out today. I think it would be best if he joins our morning excursion to Murano. By the time it's over, I bet you will have found him a lawyer. We did have two last-minute cancellations; I can say that the husband decided to come over, anyway. It's weak, I know, but hiding in plain sight is the only real option, as far as I can see."

Her boss was quiet for so long, Lana was concerned their call had been disconnected. "Dotty, are you still there?"

"Yes, I am. I don't like any of this, not one bit. But I do understand him wanting to wait to talk to the police until he has legal representation. If you think Alex joining the tour is the best option, then I guess it will have to do. Hopefully he can stay out of police custody until I can find him legal counsel."

"Fingers crossed." Lana was still mad at Alex for lying to her, but she cared far too much for him to just kick him out onto the streets or see him arrested.

"I'll put a call into my lawyer's office and get back to you soon with a name. I sure am sorry to hear that Alex is in trouble and that this horrid curse followed you to Venice."

Lana sighed into the phone. "Me, too, Dotty. Me, too."

18

Lowering the Flag

After Lana hung up the phone, she turned to Alex, expecting him to be thrilled. Instead, he looked concerned and nervous.

"I don't know, Lana. If I get caught while I'm on your tour, what are you going to say? I can't let you lose your job or possibly get arrested because of this. I should try to get out of Italy while I can. Once I'm in France or Spain, I can figure out a way to get a new passport."

"But Dotty is arranging a lawyer for you! Knowing her, she'll have a name for us by lunch. You can't just give up. And if you leave Venice, the police will only see it as evading custody, and it will make your case worse. You are going to have to wait it out."

"But where?" Alex implored.

"Great question," Lana mumbled. "You can't stay here, but you can't hang around a café or museum all day long without seeming suspicious. Besides, how would I reach you when the lawyer calls? You don't have a phone."

"You're right, I didn't think of that," he said glumly.

"As I see it, there is only one thing to do—you have to join the tour."

"Lana, the police have my passport and wallet. It's only a matter of time before they figure out I'm the person they are looking for!"

"Which is why hiding you in plain sight is the only realistic option right now. There are hundreds of tour groups meandering around the city center. If you are part of one, you'll blend right in. Once we find you a lawyer, then he or she can call the shots."

He ran a hand across Lana's cheek, murmuring, "Safety in numbers. You're a genius."

His touch made her skin feel electric. How she wished that he hadn't lied to her. She pulled away, needing to keep her distance until she could process what Alex had done. Her ex-husband had just about broken her heart when he betrayed her, and Lana didn't know whether she could take it again.

Alex got the hint and took a step back. "Okay, so what is your plan? What are you going to tell the others?"

"A married couple had to cancel at the last minute because the wife broke her hip and couldn't fly over. We can say that she was so mad that she couldn't come that she sent you—her husband—over to take lots of pictures and do some research into places to visit, so she can plan out your route for a longer trip through Italy next year."

Alex nodded. "I would buy that. And from what you have told me about previous groups, your guests tend to stick to themselves and not really mingle with the others."

"Under normal circumstances, that is true. But this group is getting along particularly well. And we have one extremely inquisitive guest, a woman named Carmen who is traveling with her friend, Rhonda. But I don't think the other members of the group will pay much you much attention."

Alex nodded before running a hand through his wavy red hair. "So what is on the agenda today?"

"Today is day five of the tour, which means we are off to the island of Murano to do a walking tour and visit a few glass factories."

"That sounds wonderful. I'll do my best to keep to the back and stay out of trouble."

"Great. Now let's get back down to the lobby. Why don't you wait a minute and then come down via the stairs? I don't want my guests to see us arriving together."

"Okay. Can I give you a kiss?"

Lana hesitated. As much as she wanted to say "yes" and throw herself into his arms, she knew that even a peck on the cheek might dissolve her resolve.

"I'll take a rain check. But thanks."

19

The Tour To Murano Must Go On

"There you are, Mr. Stevenson," Lana said loudly when Alex entered the breakfast hall. "Dotty said you would be arriving this morning."

Tom's brow furrowed. "She did?"

"Just now, when I called about Willow. She is fine, by the way. It was a phishing email."

"My wife insisted I come over to do location research," Alex said. "It's our thirtieth wedding anniversary next year and she wants to plan a monthlong trip through Italy, to celebrate."

"You'll have to take a lot of photos." Carmen's eyebrows shot up as she leaned in to study his face. "Thirty years, did you say?"

"Yes," Alex stammered. "We were high school sweethearts."

"Okay, gang, why don't we head out?" Lana said in her cheeriest of voices as she walked towards the exit.

A private water taxi transported her group across the lagoon, providing them with spectacular views of Venice on their right and Murano on their left. They sailed towards a tall white tower that shone like a beacon in the warm morning sun—Murano's lighthouse, according to their captain. The eighteen-minute trip felt shorter, and soon they were pulling into Murano's main harbor. It took a few minutes to disembark, simply because there were so many *vaporetti* and private water taxis also waiting to tie up to the docks and unload their passengers.

They followed the masses towards the island's touristic heart. Murano's Grand Canal also ran through the center of the city, its banks lined with romantic sidewalk cafés, brightly colored shops selling glass souvenirs, and signs pointing to the nearest glass factory. Lana spotted several church steeples rising above the homes and shops, adding height to the city's skyline. Several large glass installations erected in public squares also added to the city center's charm and beauty.

The seven islands that constituted Murano were linked by bridges rising high above the canals so that, Lana assumed, larger boats could pass under. Despite the busyness of the streets, the pace was more laid-back than in Venice. She soon found herself meandering instead of walking, as she craned her head to see into all of the souvenir shops they passed. Her clients were doing the same and before she knew it, her group's pace rivaled that of a snail.

Luckily, they had three hours to explore the tiny island, which gave them more than enough time to briefly see everything on their agenda. Given the close proximity of the places they were scheduled to visit, they did not have a local guide for their walk, which gave them even more flexibility. That turned out to be necessary, considering her guests did not respond to the local sights in the way that Lana had expected them to.

Their first stop—the Museo del Vetro, a museum dedicated to the art of glassmaking—was met with mixed reactions. While Carmen and Rhonda seemed intrigued by the many displays of older glass objects, the rest strolled past without really looking. The Windsor crew had already walked through the exhibition before the widowed friends had even made it halfway through. She had expected them to be more interested in the craftsmanship. But, then again, blown glass was a whole different skill set than woodworking or shipbuilding.

Alex kept to himself, loitering at the back of the group with his head down. George's expression had been switching between boredom and irritation ever since they had set foot on the island—Lana assumed thoughts of his wife were the cause.

She contemplated asking him what was the matter, but knew George would not open up to her about it. As tempted as she was to call Chrissy and check in with her, her client was an adult. And she doubted Chrissy would tell her what their fight was about over the phone. Not wanting to insert herself in the middle of a lovers' quarrel, she chose to let George be and went over to the Windsors, clustered by the exit.

"Hi, gang. Did you enjoy the exhibitions?" Lana asked.

"It's all very pretty, but museums aren't really our thing. We are here to shop, not learn about the history of glass," Kathy explained as the others nodded in agreement. The many bags already gracing their arms attested to the truth of her statement.

"Fair enough. I know I have a long list of glass figurines and vases I would love to buy as presents," Lana said. *If I can afford them*, she added in her mind. With a little luck, she could pick up something for herself, Willow, and Dotty.

"You should love the next stop—it's the basilica that you wanted to visit," she continued.

"Excellent," Harry answered. "That was my request. Their mosaics are supposed to be extraordinary. Joe and I are experimenting with using mosaic tiles as decorations. It's time-consuming, but the results are spectacular. It will be good to see how the masters did it."

Sure enough, the floors and dome of the seventh-century Basilica of Saint Mary and Saint Donatus was decorated with the most exquisite Byzantine mosaics Lana had ever seen. The Windsor crew apparently agreed and spent quite a bit of time examining and photographing the individual tiles and scenes.

Tom had to usher them back out so they would remain on schedule. Although it was primarily a walking tour, they did need to be at the glass factory on time for the demonstration Dotty had booked for them.

When their group stopped to photograph the Comet Glass Star, an abstract blue glass starburst sculpture that seemed to expand and contract in the sunlight, Lana considered checking in with Alex. However, her concern that she might treat him different than the rest made her change her mind.

Instead, she approached Tom, her fellow guide. They had three more days in Venice together, after which Dotty wanted him ready to lead a tour on his own. And especially since Lana might have to rely on him if Alex's situation worsened, she wanted to assess how receptive he'd been to her lessons these past few days.

"Hey, Tom, how are you doing?"

"It is a fascinating place. Almost like a mini-Venice," he said.

"I was thinking the same thing. Say, our guests have a free afternoon tomorrow, and most excursions require a reservation. Why don't we see if they know where they want to go, so we can get them booked in today?"

"Why don't I take care of that, Lana?"

"That would be great," she replied, happy he volunteered to take the lead on this one.

She watched as he approached George and the Windsors, who were grouped together, commiserating about Sail Away Cruises and what Matteo's death would mean for business. Lana listened as Tom inquired about their plans for tomorrow's free afternoon.

"We have heard a lot of good things about the beaches on Lido. Is there a ferry, or do we need to hire a private water taxi?" Harry asked.

Tom pulled out his phone, typed something in, and a moment later, looked back up at his guest. "I just sent you a link to the ferry schedule. But if you prefer, we can hire a private water taxi for you. Just say the word."

"Hey, thanks, Tom," Joe said and slapped him on the back.

Phew, Lana thought, *he has got this under control.* She looked to Alex and saw that he was chatting with Rhonda and Carmen. She was about to go over and ask what they wanted to do tomorrow, when she noticed that George had taken Tom aside and the two were now talking with their heads close together.

Uh, oh, what's going on now, she wondered as she moved closer to the duo.

"Chrissy and I got into a pretty nasty argument after that masquerade ball. It's my fault she's not here today. I would like to take her out to a romantic restaurant tonight and see if I can make it up to her," George said in a soft voice.

"Gosh, there are so many restaurants in Venice, I wouldn't know which one to choose," Tom said. "It's your wife—you know her better than I do.

Shouldn't you pick it?"

George's forehead creased. "Wait a second, we pay you the big bucks to take care of this kind of thing for us. Don't you have a list of recommended restaurants?" George looked around, until he made eye contact with Lana. "Maybe you can help me. Tom here is useless."

"That's a little harsh," she laughed, keeping her tone light. "This is his first tour, and I guess I still have a few things I need to share with him, such as our list of recommended restaurants. I can reserve you a table at the most romantic one at, say, eight tonight?"

George smiled and nodded. "That's perfect. Thanks, Lana."

When their client walked back over to the Windsors, Tom's glare made her pull him away from the group. "Why was Harry's request no problem, but George's was?"

"Looking up a ferry schedule is a whole lot different than picking out a romantic restaurant for someone else's wife. I don't know the lady; how am I supposed to know what she would prefer?"

"I see your point, but do you remember our talk about us being more of a personal assistant than tour guide? George is correct that the tours are expensive, and that is why our boss expects us to treat our guests like royalty. He is obviously a delegator, and in this case, we are the ones he expects to get things done. Trust me, he'll be satisfied with any on our list. I can give you a copy of it when we get back to the hotel."

"Okay," Tom said, his lips pursed. "I'll do my best to follow company guidelines."

After he stalked off in Harry's direction, Lana looked around as casually as she could, hoping to catch Alex's eye. Unfortunately, he was still deep in conversation with Carmen and Rhonda and didn't seem to notice.

As she watched them a bit longer, Lana realized that Alex did not look relaxed, but trapped. *Is Carmen interrogating him?* she wondered, figuring it was time to rescue him.

When she approached, Lana heard Rhonda ask Alex how his fictitious wife was doing.

"She's recovering quickly, thanks. If things go well, she might be able to join us in a few days."

"From a broken hip? My, that's much faster than I would have expected," Rhonda said. "Don't they take weeks, if not months, to heal?"

Alex blushed. "You're right, I'm probably being too optimistic."

"What do you think of Murano, ladies?" Lana said. Alex used the diversion to slip away from the pair.

Rhonda's face lit up. "It is incredible to see where all of this world-famous glass comes from! And visiting the shops and factory showrooms has really enlightened me to the value of this kind of art. We sell a lot of glass centerpieces and vases, thanks to Chihuly's popularity," she said, referring to the famous Pacific Northwest glass artist Dale Chihuly. "It's clear now that I have been undercharging for it! I am going to raise my prices as soon as I get home."

"That's right, you own an antiques and collectibles shop, don't you?" Lana said, glad to shift the conversation away from Alex. She turned to Carmen. "And you are an art historian?"

"I was, but I took early retirement after my husband died. I felt like life was too short to work a job I no longer found inspiring."

Rhonda clicked her tongue. "How anyone could fall out of love with art history is beyond me."

Lana, however, thought it was a shame, but understandable. From previous conversations with widowed clients, she had learned that the death of a partner often changed one's perspective on life and sometimes soured even their most intense passions.

"I stopped working because I wanted to do fun things with my time remaining," Carmen explained. "Yet I soon realized that what I really wanted was to do fun things with my husband. But it was too late. I felt myself sinking into a depression, when an invitation to our school reunion showed up on my doorstep. That's when me and Rhonda got back in touch, didn't we?"

Rhonda giggled. "We hadn't seen each other in two decades, but once we started chatting, it felt like it had only been days, not years!"

"It turned out that her husband had also recently passed. That's when we got to talking about our futures and decided to help each other check off our bucket lists. Since visiting Venice was number one on Rhonda and her husband's list, it seemed like the perfect way to start off our adventure."

"That's incredible. How wonderful that you two found each other again and that you get to travel abroad together," Lana said.

"This is the first time I've been abroad. My husband and I would have loved to travel, but we were always struggling to make ends meet. And the girls' university tuitions used up what little savings we had. My Richard always said that if money was not an issue, he would have most loved to visit Venice. That's why we are here. It's ironic that I can only afford this trip thanks to his life insurance."

Carmen hugged her friend close. "At least you get to do what he always wanted to do, even if it's with me, instead."

"Luckily, most of the items on our bucket lists are not as expensive as a week in Venice." Rhonda pulled out of her friend's embrace and wiped her eyes dry. "And we are both young enough that we don't need to rush things."

"That's true, though I am more of a sooner-than-later-kind of gal," Carmen replied.

"You know I'm not giving up my shop, so you are going to have to be patient."

"Oh, so you are not thinking of retiring anytime soon, Rhonda?" Lana asked.

"No way. I'm going to keep my shop open as long as I'm physically able. It's my passion, and it pays the bills. My husband's insurance has made things easier, but I'm only fifty-two years old, and I have a lot of life left in me still. I also know from my mother-in-law's experience that the older you get, the more expensive your medical care is. I used to drive her up to Canada to fill her prescriptions, otherwise she couldn't afford all of the medicines keeping her alive!"

"It is tough," Lana murmured, recalling other clients, even ones whom she considered to be quite wealthy, complaining about their high medical costs.

Her beeping telephone broke up their conversation. "Oops, sorry about that, ladies. My telephone is reminding me that it is time for a quick snack before our factory tour."

20

Placing Bets

After she found them a spot at an adorable café, its windows trimmed with flowering vines, her clients shared their thoughts about their whirlwind tour of Murano. All seemed enchanted by the prettiness of the place, yet were surprised by how compact it was.

"It is really cute, and you only need a morning to see it all. It's the perfect day trip," Kathy said to her husband, who nodded in agreement, his mouth too full of sandwich to respond with words.

"It is smaller than I had expected, and a whole lot busier," Carmen said.

"But the glass!" Rhonda exclaimed. "It is heavenly!"

After polishing off their snack of *polpette* or fried meatballs, *tramezzini* or triangle-shaped sandwiches, and a selection of pickled vegetables, her group was sated and happy.

"Is everyone ready to go?" Tom asked, just as Lana wanted to do the same. *He is getting into the swing of things, after all*, she thought.

George licked his fingers clean. "You bet. Are we heading back to Venice?"

"Not yet. We have a glass-blowing demonstration to attend first. We'll head back to Saint Mark's Square afterwards," Tom explained.

"Alright," George grumbled. Lana figured his sullen attitude had to do with the fact that this was what his wife had wanted to see the most. If they did make up before the tour ended, she would have to arrange a private water taxi for them to visit Murano together.

Tom led them over to a nondescript building, decorated only with the name of the factory painted across its front doors. The inside harbored a showroom filled with glass objects that any museum would be envious of. They walked slowly through the busy space, taking in the colorful dishes, glasses, vases, centerpieces, and figurines. Some pieces were striped or transparent, and others were a swirl of cloud-like colors. Most were protected by glass display cases, though some were mounted onto pedestals. Those were the larger centerpieces and vases, though no one in their right mind would actually put a flower in them—they were far too beautiful in their own right.

"I can't wait to see how they blow the glass," Rhonda gushed, reminding Lana that they had to check in for their tour.

After explaining that Murano's glass tradition was thanks to the Doge of Venice, who had ordered all of the city's furnaces to be moved to Murano in 1291 as a precaution against fire, the salesperson ushered them towards the demonstration. They entered through a set of large metal doors that Lana imaged a double-decker bus could easily pass through. Inside the hangar-like hall were four enormous furnaces.

"One of our glass blowers will take you through the process of creating a vase. Enjoy the demonstration," the saleslady said before returning to the showroom.

Lana and her clients joined the forty tourists already standing in a semi-circle that had been marked off with red and white tape. On the other side stood the massive ovens, each with a tiny window-shaped door. One was open, giving them a glimpse into the bowels of the furnace, an angry red-orange mass of shimmering light and heat.

A few moments later, a middle-aged man entered from a door on the other side of the tape. In his hand was a long, metal rod with a blob of transparent glass wrapped around the end of it.

Without a word, he thrust the pipe into the open door, far into the sea of flames. When he took it out again, the blob was now glowing as brightly as the oven's interior. The man immediately began shaping and pulling the glowing glass with metal pliers. When the red seemed to lighten to orange, the glass master returned it to the furnace until it heated up again, then repeated the procedure. Several times, he dipped the glowing glass into a powdery substance, then returned it to the oven. When he pulled it back out, the blob had changed in color. After several dips, swirls of red, blue, and purple began to emerge.

When he blew through the open metal rod and the glass billowed out like a ball, he cut it open and then pulled and twisted it, extending its length and breadth. His hand continually spun the rod to ensure the shape didn't collapse. The glass master did not speak the entire time they were in the room, but his hands were in nonstop motion. It was mesmerizing watching him work.

After he had finished the piece, he held the large vase up so everyone could see it, before laying the pipe down across a workbench and slicing the glass object off with a single cut. To Lana, it seemed like he had captured clouds of color in the glass.

"I have to buy one of those!" Rhonda exclaimed, to which the rest of her guests agreed. When the glass master carried his creation to the gift shop, she added, "Or perhaps I can buy the one he just made."

Rhonda scurried off, just ahead of the pack.

The pieces inside the shop were as beautifully displayed as those in the factory's showroom. The many free-standing cases showed off the enormous vases, centerpieces, and figurines similar to those Lana had seen decorating their hotel, as well as the more expensive restaurants and shops they had visited.

To her relief, there were also many smaller pieces for sale, but her hopes were quickly dashed when she noted the prices. Even a tiny ornament would exceed her budget. Lana watched with a twinge of jealousy as the Windsors walked over to the checkout counter with a basket full of glasses, figurines, and vases.

After settling for a wine-bottle stopper topped with an abstract starburst, Lana decided to check in with her guests. Alex had pulled his hat even lower over his forehead and was wandering slowly around the room, turning to avoid the many security cameras as he went. George seemed indifferent as he stared into space. Lana could imagine he was thinking of Chrissy right now. This was the place she had wanted to visit most, and it was thanks to their fight that she had not joined them.

At least he seems to be showing remorse, Lana thought. He did want to book a romantic restaurant for them tonight—that was a start.

The Windsor crew stood by the door, bags in hand, apparently ready to leave. Rhonda and Carmen were standing in front of a large display case filled with gondolas in a variety of sizes. Lana joined them, curious to see how the glassblowers had re-created the classic shape. The gondolas were blown from one long piece of glass that was deep black in the middle and slightly transparent on the ends. Even the tiniest of boats featured a gondolier, complete with hat, striped shirt, and oar, standing at the back. The larger examples had a heart-shaped chair complete with kissing clients inside. Each piece had been crafted out of glass and then melted onto the rest.

"I wonder if the police have found Matteo's gondola yet," Rhonda said to her traveling companion.

"It will be interesting to see whether the environmentalists stole it when they killed Matteo," Carmen added.

"My money is on that little man from the museum," Rhonda grumbled. "He was so rude! At the party he was so protective of the statue that I never did get a chance to really look at it up close. And then there was that whole business with the water taxi after the party. I still don't understand why we couldn't share the ride."

Carmen tapped her chin a moment before answering. "Unless he didn't want us to know where he was going."

"Why would that matter?"

"What if it was not the environmentalist who stole the gondola?" Carmen countered. "What if the museum representative had the water taxi drop him off around the corner, then walked back and stole the statue? He had an invitation to the party, so he could have gotten into the building without raising any suspicions. And he knew that the gondola was up in Matteo's office. The guy must have known that he would have to wait another year to get close to it again—short of a court injunction."

"But how did he get into the safe?" Lana asked, inserting herself into the conversation. "Sorry for eavesdropping, but I think your theory is intriguing." Even though she really did not know whether Carmen's theory was plausible, if suspicion could be diverted from the environmentalists, then Alex stood a better chance of convincing the police that he did not kill Matteo.

"I guess the better question is, who put the gondola back in the safe?" Carmen asked.

"Matteo told Vittoria to do it—and in a degrading way," Lana replied, as a thought struck. "She did seem pretty bitter about losing out on the CEO position, and she knew that Matteo loved that gondola. Could she have taken it, simply to hurt him? It would have been petty of her, but then, she had just lost out on a major promotion. Come to think of it, if she had really wanted to make Matteo mad, she could have given it to the museum representative."

Rhonda's eyes about bulged out of her head. "Carmen! You see everything—did that museum guy have a bag with him, when we saw him on the dock waiting for the taxi? Maybe he snuck it out of the party and that was why he didn't want us tagging along—in case we saw it."

Her friend shook her head. "No, and there's no way he could have hidden it under his waistcoat without us noticing. The statue was far too long and bulky."

"That's too bad," Rhonda said, echoing Lana's thoughts.

"And that still wouldn't explain who killed Matteo," Lana added.

"But that doesn't mean that Vittoria didn't steal it," Carmen replied. "If I was in her shoes, I would have been extremely upset and may have lashed out and done something stupid."

"I do like the idea about Vittoria being involved with the theft. And she did tell the police that she was on the upper floor when the cleaning lady spotted the, ah, suspect running out of Matteo's office," Lana said. She had almost said Alex's name.

"You know what this means, don't you?" Carmen looked to Lana and Rhonda. "The police may be dealing with two different crimes. The boat's theft may have nothing to do with the break-in or protest."

She hesitated a moment, as if considering the possibilities, when her brow furrowed. "Or the boat may be the cause of it all. If Matteo was killed during a robbery gone wrong, it might make it even more difficult for the police to unmask the real killer."

"Great," Lana muttered.

"I guess we will have to wait and see what the police come up with," Rhonda added, in a cheery tone.

Though Lana usually found her guest's voice to be delightful, right now, her flippancy grated on her nerves.

21

Mistaken Identity

Their conversation made Lana's thoughts turn again to Alex's predicament. She looked around the showroom, needing to see how he was doing. She finally spotted him standing at the back of the space, gazing intently into a display case. Lana excused herself and walked casually over, making sure to keep a respectable distance between them. The last thing she wanted was for her clients to think that she was flirting with the new guest.

"How are you holding up?" Lana asked, without moving her lips. She hoped Alex could understand her garbled question.

Before he could answer, Tom bounced over. "Excuse me, but the Windsor crew would like to leave. Should I take them to a café for a drink, or ask if the rest are ready to leave, as well?"

Lana looked at her watch, shocked to see it was already twelve-thirty. "Gosh, we should get back to the *vaporetto*, actually. We have lunch reservations in an hour back on Venice island."

"Great, thanks, Lana." Tom squeezed her shoulder before walking back to Dave, Kathy, Harry, and Joe.

"You two are on good terms," Alex said through pursed lips.

His comment riled her up. How dare he question her loyalty, especially considering all she was doing to help him?

"He's one of the most arrogant men I have ever met, but he will make a great guide, once he learns to treat the guests with more respect. Why, are you jealous? I thought you trusted me to tell you the whole truth and not leave anything crucial out."

Even without making eye contact, Lana could feel how she wounded him. A sigh escaped her lips. "Sorry, that was petty. We need to head back to Venice now. I have to round up the other guests," she said softly, before adding in a much louder voice, "Could you please join the Windsors, Mr. Stevenson? We'll be leaving in just a moment."

Once outside, Tom took the lead, moving swiftly through the busy streets. Her guests weaved in and out of the thick crowds, stopping on occasion to point out a glass trinket or pretty viewpoint to their companions.

He's almost ready to lead a tour on his own, but not quite, Lana grumbled internally, when she noticed that Tom was far ahead of the rest and didn't appear to be slowing down.

"Hey, Tom," she called out, "could you slow down? Our guests can't keep up."

Tom stopped and turned to look for their clients, using his hand to shield his eyes from the bright sun. Between the crowds, jovial chitchat, and all the window shopping going on, it was slow going. The Windsor crew was almost a block behind him. Trailing after them were George and Alex. But Lana didn't see Carmen and Rhonda ahead of her.

Did I pass them and not see them? she wondered. It wouldn't be a surprise if she had; the streets were packed full of tourists moving in both directions. Luckily, Carmen was tall enough that Lana spotted her quickly. She had indeed passed them by. Before Lana could double back, she noted that both women were turning away from a window display they had been gesturing at and were now walking towards her.

She waited by an open door, only realizing that it was a tiny café when the strong scent of freshly ground coffee reached her nostrils. Lana looked longingly inside, wondering how long it would take the barista to make an espresso, when she noticed a television hanging above the bar. New video footage of the break-in at Sail Away Cruises was playing on a loop. Lana froze as Alex's face filled the screen.

His portrait was courtesy of a security camera hanging on a building across

118

the canal from Sail Away Cruises' headquarters. The photo appeared to be a still-frame capture of a video image, and therefore was grainy and slightly blurred. However, to Lana, Alex was instantly recognizable.

They didn't release his name; he still might be able to get out of the country, she thought, until reality came crashing down. *Only if the customs officer is blind.*

Because Alex was a suspect in a murder case, his photo would surely be distributed to all train stations, airports, and ferry terminals. And if the police had taken his suitcase with his wallet and passport inside, then it was only a matter of time before they put a name to the face.

She glanced over at her boyfriend, waiting with Tom and the rest a block away. What she wouldn't give to throw her arms around him and hug him tight! But she knew that she could not do so in front of her clients.

When Rhonda and Carmen finally caught up, Lana rushed forward, hoping the pair would not notice the breaking news story as they walked past. So far, Carmen had proved to be extremely observant, and she didn't want her to unmask Alex before Dotty could arrange a lawyer for him.

Unfortunately, Carmen stopped in front of the open door and stood transfixed as she stared inside the dark space.

Lana slowed her pace but didn't stop, hoping the two would get the hint and catch up. Rhonda kept moving, but Carmen remained stock still. "Hey, Lana," she called out a few seconds later. "Could you come here for a moment?"

Lana's heart sank as she doubled back to her client.

"Are you certain that new guest is who he says he is?"

"What do you mean?" Lana whispered, struggling to keep her voice even.

Carmen pointed at the television screen. "Mr. Stevenson sure does look like that activist the police are searching for."

Lana finally turned and acknowledged the television screen. She didn't need to understand Italian to follow along. The security video footage of her boyfriend and five others rappelling down the face of the Sail Away offices and running off into the night was as clear as day. The close-up of Alex's face that they kept visible in one corner of the screen, along with the "breaking news" banner across the bottom, made clear that he was in a whole lot of trouble.

When she turned to Carmen, she noticed that Alex was now hovering behind them. Based on his widened eyes and paling face, she figured he could see the television, as well. Their eyes locked briefly—his gaze was so haunted that it took all of Lana's willpower not to wrap her arms around him. Instead, she motioned for him to get back to the rest.

Lana made a point of studying the screen for a long time before answering. "I see what you mean. The resemblance is strong, but it can't be him. Mr. Stevenson flew in this morning, after the ball took place. Don't they say we all have a doppelganger somewhere on this planet?" Lana laughed.

"I guess so..." Carmen's voice trailed off as she chewed on her lip. But her feet remained planted in front of the television screen.

Lana looked towards the others, before exclaiming, "Gosh, the group is quite a ways ahead. Shall we catch up? We have lunch reservations at a wonderful café close to our hotel. It would be a shame to miss it," she said lightly as she moved on, ignoring Carmen's protests.

Only when the crowd bottlenecked close to the marina and they had slowed to a snail's pace did Lana dare maneuver her way over to Alex. In the thick crowd, she hoped no one from her group would notice them talking. "We need to get you a scarf to cover up more of your face."

"What happened back there with Carmen?" he whispered.

"She recognized you from the news, but I think I convinced her that you are not him."

"That's bad, Lana. If she saw through my disguise..."

She nodded, blinking back the tears. "I know." She bit her lip and looked away. "I have to get the group back to our hotel for a quick break before lunch. I think you better hide out in my room until Dotty calls with a lawyer's name. The cleaners should be done with it by now."

Alex nodded then moved towards the middle of their group and cast his head downwards. They were, after all, pretending to be nothing more than client and guide.

22

A Few Discrepancies

On the boat ride back, Lana took in the splendid views, hoping Venice's beauty would quell the ball of fear growing in her stomach. Looking out over the water like this, from the safety of their boat, she could momentarily forget her worries. There was something quite special about chugging along the choppy water so low that the historical buildings seemed to rise up out of the blue-green soup. As they sailed close to the ancient buildings, the tower and twin columns slowly came into view, appearing as a *fata morgana* in the warm sunlight.

Her group was spaced out in a long, yet narrow, boat, hired to transport them back and forth from the main island to Murano. The guests took advantage of the spacious accommodations, spreading out so everyone was seated next to a window, leaving the center aisle empty.

Alex had positioned himself by the exit, away from the rest. As far as she could tell, Carmen was the only one who had seen the television news, and no one else seemed to be paying him any mind.

Lana sat across the aisle from him, making sure to keep her body half-turned away. Carmen was definitely one of the more observant clients she had had on a tour, but she didn't want to give the others a reason to suspect anything.

As they approached Saint Mark's Square, the sun reflecting off of the winged lion transformed the mythical beast into a beacon of light. When her guests reached for their cameras, Lana dared to catch his eye and smile slightly.

As much as his lies hurt her, she was starting to see that his deceit was of a whole other order than her ex-husband's. Alex had not betrayed their bond, but had chosen to hide a part of himself. Yes, the protests could be dangerous, but he said he had only taken part in two, and the rest of the time, he worked behind the scenes. His passion for rock climbing was far more dangerous. If he found the volunteer work inspiring, why should she try to stop him from taking part?

Lana glanced at Alex when the boat slowed, fearing they still had a lot to discuss before things would go back to how they were before he joined the Earth Warriors. His sunglasses made it impossible to read his emotions, but she could imagine that he was terrified. How she wished she could do something more to comfort him.

He had said that he craved more adventure in his life, but this was certainly not the kind he was referring to. Could it be that their relationship was simply too boring for him, she wondered. She wasn't yet forty, but because she spent most of her time with folks in their sixties and seventies, she feared that she was starting to act older than her years, even when she was not on tour duty. Lana racked her brain, yet couldn't recall the last time she and Alex had done something crazy or off the wall together. The mini-vacations they enjoyed between jobs were lightning-fast visits to Europe's largest cities, where the craziest thing they did together was splurge on an expensive bottle of wine.

No, this isn't on me, she thought as a surge of anger rose up from within. She knew that if the situation was reversed, she would not have hidden anything from him. Alex was the one who didn't trust her enough to tell her the truth. *I'm not at fault here, he is. And until he apologizes for that, I don't know how we will get past this.*

Lana looked outside and noticed they were fast approaching the dock. As much as she wanted to talk everything out with him, now was not the time, Lana realized as she took another sidelong glance at her partner. After Dotty called with a lawyer's name, Alex would turn himself in, and they would all pray that justice would be served and he would be released. In the meantime, she had a tour to lead.

After disembarking, it was a short walk to the hotel. On the way, she explained to her guests that they had a fifteen-minute break to freshen up, before they were requested to return to the hotel lobby so that they could walk over to a famous bistro for lunch.

After they entered the lobby, a group of uniformed officers stood to greet them. When Detective Esposito stepped towards her, Lana sensed that they might be late for their meal.

Her heart rate doubled as she smiled at the detective. "Hello, Detective. Can we help you with anything?" Out of the corner of her eye, she saw Alex step back behind Tom, hiding most of his body from the detective's gaze.

"Good afternoon, Miss Hansen. I don't mean to interrupt your sightseeing, but we have a few questions for several members of your group. We hope to clear them up here, instead of having to escort you all to the station. Can we all sit down and have a chat about the party?"

Lana looked to her clients, all of whom seemed as shocked by the detective's subtle threat as she was. "Certainly."

"Why don't we talk at the back." The detective gestured towards the far corner of the lobby where several wingback chairs had been arranged in a half-circle.

How long have the police been here, waiting for us to return? Lana wondered. She waved Tom and the rest of her group forward, daring to whisper to Alex, "It's better to stay put for now, I'm afraid," once the others had moved forward.

As much as she wanted to tell him to run up to her room, she figured that his departure would seem suspicious. The officers stood in a row that he would have to walk through, in order to reach the staircase leading up to her room. And his getup was already suspect enough. His sunglasses and floppy hat did seem rather ridiculous considering they were inside, but she knew it was better for him to keep them on.

Her boyfriend nodded slightly before taking a seat in one corner, half hidden behind George's ample frame.

"Let me be candid," the detective began, locking eyes with all in his audience before continuing. "We have interviewed more than two hundred individuals present at the Sail Away party, and it took quite a bit of time to compile all of the statements. Now that our team has done so, we have a much better idea of who was where when Matteo Conti's body was discovered. We are now following up on a few, shall we say, discrepancies between witnesses statements."

Lana's eyebrows knitted together as she looked up at the tall officer. "What do you mean, discrepancies?"

The detective smiled but did not answer, instead shifting his gaze back to her clients. To Lana's relief, his gaze fell specifically on George and the Windsor crew.

"I see you eyeing me. Let's get this over with. What do you want to know?" George said in a gruff tone that Lana found inappropriate when dealing with the police.

"Very observant, Mr. Fretwell. According to your original statement, you were standing at the bar, sipping a drink, when Matteo Conti's body was discovered."

"Yeah?" George crossed his arms over his ample belly.

"And you, David Windsor, and your employee, Harry"—the detective nodded to both men—"also said that you were downstairs at the time."

Harry leaned forward, his large frame making his dark expression seem even more menacing. "That's right."

Dave nodded, though his expression seemed less certain than that of his employee.

"Several witness statements confirm that all three of you went upstairs to speak to Matteo Conti shortly before he was murdered. And all of you were seen in the vicinity of Mr. Conti's office when the body was discovered."

"Wait a moment—who said that we were up there?" Harry challenged.

"A member of the cleaning crew."

George laughed. "Really? How does she know who we are? I don't think I have any Venetian cleaners as clients at my investment brokerage."

It was the detective's turn to sound smug. "Do you recall that my officers took photographs of your passports? We had more than one reason to do so."

"That sounds illegal to me," George countered.

The officer shook his head. "Not if it helps us to find a killer—or perhaps killers."

The three men's faces drained of color.

"Now wait a second," George protested, "I did go up to talk to Matteo and was on the top floor when that lady began screaming bloody murder, but I was still in the hallway, trying to locate his office. I guess it's a good thing I didn't find it, otherwise you really would have thought I was involved with his murder. But I'm not. Go ahead and take my fingerprints—you won't find any traces of me in there."

"Why did you want to speak to the deceased?"

George's face turned crimson. "It's a private matter."

The inspector scanned the small group, studying the women's faces before turning his attention back to George. "Where is your lovely wife?"

"At the spa. Why do you want to speak to her?"

"Some of the discrepancies involve her statement, as well."

George's jaw contracted as his fists began to clench.

The inspector must have noticed, too. "Why don't we step over to that corner, where we can discuss this more privately. Or you can accompany me to the police station, if you prefer."

"Over there is fine." George hefted his heavy frame up and out of the chair, then followed the inspector over to the opposite side of the lobby.

Lana and the rest watched their animated conversation, but she could not figure out what they were discussing based on their body language alone.

"I bet you ten bucks that Chrissy was in Matteo's office when he was killed," Carmen whispered to Rhonda.

How could she be? Lana thought, Chrissy wanted to leave the party because she didn't want to run into Matteo again. So why would she have gone up to his office?

"That's probably why the police want to speak to her, too," Rhonda agreed.

What if Carmen's right? Lana wondered. What if Chrissy lied, and George had found them up in Matteo's office together? Before she could work out the potential implications for Alex, she noticed her boyfriend shifting uncomfortably in his seat.

Lana's brow furrowed, until she noticed one of the younger officers staring at Alex. She tried to push down the wave of terror coursing through her veins and stepped as casually as she could in between the two men, attempting to block the officer's view. With his floppy hat pulled far down over his wraparound sunglasses, Alex did look quite outlandish.

She put on her most confident grin. "Officer, if you don't mind me asking, one of my clients is looking for a really romantic restaurant here in Venice. Could you possibly recommend one?" She batted her eyes and coquettishly placed a hand on her hip, hoping her attempts at flirting with the much younger man—in the middle of an interrogation, no less—didn't come across as absurd. Not that it mattered how silly she looked; as long as the policeman forgot about her boyfriend, it didn't matter what he thought of her.

"*Si,*" the man replied immediately and pulled out his phone to show her where his favorite was. "There are so many to choose from, but this one"—he pointed to a café close to Rialto Bridge—"is where I proposed to my wife. To me, it's the most romantic place in the city."

Lana noted the address and thanked the officer, glad to see that the inspector was turning back towards the group.

When he and George returned, her client was far more humble than she had ever seen him. Based on how he kept his head down and his gaze low, whatever they had discussed had obviously been painful for him.

As George took a seat, the inspector looked to Dave and Harry. "Would you also prefer to speak in private?"

The two men exchanged glances before shaking their heads.

"No, but we should come clean. We were not entirely honest with you." Dave sighed.

"Sail Away Cruises is three months late with their final payment of a fleet of ocean-going vessels that Matteo personally ordered from our boat-building company." Dave grabbed his wife's hand and kissed it before continuing, "Matteo refused to answer any of our phone calls or emails, which is why we flew over, to see if we could find out what the holdup was. During his speech last night, he told the crowd how Sail Away Cruises was shifting its focus to riverboat cruises, and he hinted that they were going to be working with one of our main European competitors, instead of us."

"We were livid," Kathy added. "After his speech, we confronted him about it, and Matteo confirmed that, because of the company's shift, he was not going to pay for the fleet he ordered from us. What kind of businessman does something like that?"

The detective nodded along, urging them to continue.

Dave wrung his hands, avoiding the officer's gaze as he spoke. "After we talked to our competitor and he confirmed that he'd signed a contract with Sail Away Cruises for a new fleet of riverboats, Harry and me went upstairs to give Matteo a piece of our mind."

"Your what?" the inspector asked, the idiom apparently exceeding his grasp of English.

"We were angry at how he treated us and wanted to make sure he knew it," Dave explained. "But we did not kill Matteo. In fact, we didn't even see him! We'd just stepped into the hallway on the top floor when that cleaning lady raced past us, screaming her lungs out."

"Why did you lie to me last night?"

"Because we didn't want you to see us as suspects. I suppose, because we were up there, we could have done it. But we did not! Like George said, you can take our fingerprints or a lock of hair, but you won't find any trace of us in his office."

"If it helps, I don't think the killer escaped via the staircase because they would have had to run past us to reach it," Harry added.

"No," the investigator said dryly, "he rappelled down to the street, jumped into a speedboat, and escaped before our police boats could arrive."

Lana's eyes automatically flickered towards her boyfriend. Speedboats and police chases? Who was this man seated across from her?

23

Walking the Plank

After snapping his notepad shut, the inspector bowed to Lana's group. "Thank you for your cooperation. We may be in touch later, if we have more questions about this crime. Until then, I hope you enjoy our beautiful city."

He stepped back to make room for her group to walk past him and his officers. Lana willed her clients to hot-foot it out of there, but not all of them seemed to have received her mental message.

"Did you find the gondola yet?" Rhonda blurted out when she passed the detective.

His brow furrowed as he looked to his junior officers for enlightenment. When they shrugged, he turned back to the pair of friends. "Excuse me?"

"The statue of the gondola that Matteo was going to donate to the museum. It's worth a small fortune, and it disappeared last night. Its theft has been reported on in a few of the local newspapers."

"It might not be the environmentalists, after all. Matteo's death might have been part of a robbery gone wrong. It wouldn't be the first time, you know," Carmen added.

Instead of looking taken aback, the officer smiled widely and spoke a little louder, as if he was addressing two slightly deaf great-aunts he had not seen in years. "*Signora*, Italy has an incredible art division, dedicated to such crimes. They have been informed of the gondola's disappearance. My team is too busy trying to solve a murder to worry about an art theft."

"But perhaps the gondola is why he was killed," Carmen pushed. "The museum representative was quite rude to us after the party."

"So that makes him a killer?" The detective's smile and tone grew weary; Lana could see he was rapidly losing his patience with the pair. She was also losing her mind with worry, hoping the two friends would let the gondola go, so that the police would leave before one of them recognized Alex's face.

"I suppose that's not really conclusive proof," Rhonda conceded.

"*Signora*, if you will excuse me, we have a long list of discrepancies to clarify today. Enjoy your time in Venice."

Lana felt a surge of relief when the two ladies moved forward. Until the young officer spoke again.

"Is it too bright for you?" he asked, a smile tugging on his lips as he gestured towards Alex's sunglasses.

Too late. Lana pinched herself, to suppress a cry.

"I'm afraid I had too much to drink last night, I've got a killer headache," Alex said sheepishly.

The young officer laughed. "I've been there."

Their brief exchange made the detective turn and study Alex's face. "Sir, could you remove your sunglasses, please?"

Alex's hands trembled as he lowered his shades. Before they reached his nose, the detective sucked in his breath. "Alex Wright," was all he said, but the two words made his colleagues turn and tense up. Lana could see the glimmer of recognition in the officers' eyes.

How could they know his name? she thought, frozen in place.

Before she or the officers could react, Alex bolted for the front door.

The policemen chased after him, with her group right on their heels. Outside, several tourists snapping photos of the gorgeous views blocked his path. When one officer was close enough to grab his arm, Alex jumped over a suitcase and landed on his knee, right next to the edge of the canal. Lana could see him scanning the water's surface before he sprang towards a postal boat moving rapidly past, just as two officers grabbed at his shirt.

Unfortunately, he misjudged the distance and fell into the water with a loud splash.

"Alex!" Lana screamed, terrified he would be chopped up by the boat's propellers.

To her relief, he quickly bobbed to the surface, and the wake pushed him back to the canal's edge.

"I am innocent!" Alex sputtered as the officers fished him out. "That man was already dead when I found him."

"Then why did you run away from the scene and continue to elude capture?" the inspector raged. "You must have seen the news reports making clear that we were searching for you. If you are innocent, you would have turned yourself in straight away."

Lana smashed her fists against her forehead. Dotty was right—no good would come from waiting. The police were going to assume Alex did it, unless his lawyer could prove otherwise.

24

Killer In Their Midst

Lana watched silently as the officer helped her boyfriend step into the police boat. She bit her lip to avoid calling out his name again. The last thing they needed was for her to draw attention to herself and also be taken in for questioning.

Alex glanced back in her direction, a terrified look in his eye, but he didn't try to speak to her.

Lana lowered her head, glad her hair was long enough to hide her face. She didn't want her clients to see the tears she couldn't stop from rolling down her cheeks. Several deep breaths helped her stop the flow, after which she discreetly wiped her face dry with a Kleenex. When she turned around, Lana saw that her group was clustered together out on the sidewalk, watching the drama play out.

Get it together, girl. You have to do this for Dotty, Lana told herself. How she wished that she was working with Randy Wright on this tour. He was one of the most trustworthy and easygoing co-workers she had ever had. On the other hand, Alex was his big brother, and if Randy was here right now, he would be far too emotional to lead any tour.

As much as she wanted to take an hour off to get her emotions under control, Lana knew she could not. Right now, she had to get them to the restaurant for lunch. As experienced as Tom was, Lana could not yet trust him to be alone with the group. If she did take time off and something happened to one of their guests because they didn't get the help they needed in time, she would never forgive herself.

Lana had to trust that her boss would find Alex a suitable lawyer who could get him out of this mess. Now, she had to return the favor and do her job without complaint, knowing that it was the best way to help her boyfriend.

She sucked in a lungful of air and blew it out quickly before plastering on a smile and turning back to her group.

"How did we not know that we had a killer in our midst?" Joe asked.

Tom shook his head as he watched the police boat speed away. "You never would have guessed that he was a murderer. That guy seemed so normal."

"You always hear about that on the news, that somebody's neighbor was a serial killer and nobody noticed," Harry added.

Suddenly Lana noticed that Carmen was watching her slyly out of the corner of her eye. *Shoot, did she hear me call out Alex's name?* she wondered.

"Lana, was that guy really the missing guest? His story about his wife sending him on vacation alone didn't ring true to me," Kathy said.

She shrugged off the question.

"Have you had murderers on your tours before? Is this typical for a Wanderlust tour?" George pushed.

Lana blanched, unwilling to answer that question honestly.

"What are the odds that the husband flew over to kill Matteo and then joined the tour? He must have been an imposter. Though one familiar with Wanderlust Tour's itinerary. And how did he know that the couple canceled at the last minute?" Carmen persisted.

She is far too perceptive, Lana thought. "It is a mystery," she said aloud, "and one my boss will definitely want me to solve. But now, it's time for lunch."

"Gosh, I am famished," Rhonda piped up, to Lana's relief. She strode ahead, knowing her group would follow along. As she walked, Lana swore she could feel Carmen's eyes boring into her back.

25

A Grand View Over the Canal

The views from the Ponte dell'Accademia were spectacular. It was as if Venice was showing off, in an attempt to distract Lana from her negative thoughts. Her group was standing atop the steep wooden structure, snapping picture after picture of the Grand Canal as it flowed into Saint Mark's Basin. It was truly a glorious sight, and rightfully one of the most photographed spots in Venice.

Ahead on their right, the Santa Maria della Salute, a white domed church at the mouth of the canal, seemed to shimmer in the warm sunlight. Tall poles painted in curving red and white stripes that reminded Lana of barber's poles marked the ends of the many piers sticking out into the canal. The blue-green waters were filled with a plethora of small transport boats, *vaporetti*, luxurious yachts, and many gondolas, all riding the choppy waves. The lagoon was filled with so many boats that Lana bet she could hop from one side to the other without getting wet.

Behind the watercraft rose elegant palazzos, richly decorated villas with lattice-carved stone screens, Gothic statues, curvaceous balconies, and multipaned windows that reflected the warm light back over the water in sun-streaked ripples. These were home to Venice's richest residents. Through open curtains, Lana caught glimpses of chandeliers made of Murano glass and expensive-looking pieces of art filling these magnificent private residences. She momentarily dreamed of living in such a luxurious space, wondering whether it would feel like it was home or like a museum.

Partially hidden behind several large trees was the Peggy Guggenheim Collection. The distinctive modern structure was one of the only ones to have a private garden along this canal that was not hidden away by high stone walls. Lana couldn't wait to visit it tomorrow morning and get a better look at both the incredible artwork it was supposed to house, as well as the fabulous-looking garden.

On previous tours, she had always drawn comfort from their visits to Europe's most important monuments to culture and the arts. She hoped the Guggenheim would have the same effect.

Her life was becoming a surreal nightmare, one she had little control over. Instead of continually scolding herself for not forcing Alex to surrender to the police as soon as he knocked on her hotel room door, she had to let it go. There was nothing she could do but wait until Dotty called. Now that Alex was in police custody, the only person who could prove his innocence was the lawyer Dotty would soon provide him with. Instead of succumbing to her depression, Lana chose to take in the beauty before her, hoping it would help to calm her soul.

Her phone began ringing as she took another snapshot. She answered it quickly and stepped away from her group. Before she could utter a word, the caller began speaking in a bubbly voice.

"Help is on its way," Dotty announced. "I just got word from my legal team that a law firm close to your hotel is prepared to help Alex. The lawyer can pick him up and take him straight to the nearest police station. Where is he now?"

"It's too late," Lana cried. "The police have arrested him."

"Oh, darling, I'm sorry to hear that. You better call the lawyer and let him get started. His name is Salvatore Romano," Dotty said before relaying his telephone number.

After giving Lana a minute to jot it down, Dotty added, "Mr. Romano comes highly recommended. Apparently, he is Italian but graduated from Berkeley and worked in California for a number of years. My lawyers tell me his English is perfect. I've already asked that he hire a private investigator, as well, so you don't feel the need to do any sleuthing of your own. I can imagine you want to help Alex in any way you can, but the best thing you can do is stay out of it."

Something about the seriousness of Dotty's tone made Lana shiver. Her boss was usually a jovial, cheery person who could see the best in any situation. "What's going on? You're scaring me a little."

"Well, good, because my lawyers scared the bejesus out of me when I told them who Alex was accused of murdering. Matteo wasn't the charming businessman I thought he was, Lana. It sure sounds like he made a lot of enemies on the way up, and I don't want you getting caught up in any of that."

"Do you mean, like, Mafia stuff?" Lana whispered into the phone, terrified a local might hear her say the *M* word aloud.

"I don't know about that. But he is involved in several lawsuits with companies across Europe and the United States. It sounds like he was the kind of man who regularly skirted the line between legal and illegal and was used to using any means necessary to get away with it."

"What has Alex gotten himself mixed up in?" Lana cried.

"I do not know," Dotty murmured.

"Okay, I think I understand the situation. Thanks again for finding Alex legal counsel," Lana replied, her mind already running through her conversation with the lawyer.

"Honey, you don't sound scared, so I don't think you do. I need you to promise me that you will keep your nose out of the investigation. Can you do that—for me and Alex?"

Lana sucked in her breath. "Trust me, I am more than happy to leave the investigating to your lawyer and his PI. I've already gotten into more trouble than I would have liked on previous tours. I'm grateful someone else can champion Alex's cause right now."

"Are you going to be able to do your job?" Dotty asked in a far gentler tone. "I would send over another guide to take your place, but there are only three more days to the tour. By the time I found you a replacement and they flew over, the tour would be practically finished."

"No," Lana said, a touch too forcefully. Though she wasn't planning on doing any investigation *per se*, she couldn't help but think of her guests who had been questioned twice now by the police. If one of them was involved in the crime, then she owed it to Alex to find out which one. And the only way that was going to happen was if she kept leading the tour.

"It will be a challenge, but the tour must go on. And I would prefer to stay in Venice and be close to Alex. That way the lawyer can keep me updated," Lana replied, allowing her emotions to bubble to the surface.

"Okay, darling. You hang in there. This lawyer is supposed to be one of the best in Italy, so you should be in good hands. Trust me, he's not cheap, but Alex is worth every penny. You just sit tight and let his team take care of your boyfriend."

Lana breathed out a sigh of relief. "Thanks, Dotty. Just knowing that there is a professional looking out for Alex is already a huge relief. I'll give the lawyer a call as soon as I get my group settled at the restaurant."

26

Confession Time

After her conversation with Dotty, Lana approached Tom and asked him to lead the group to the café. It wasn't a long walk, but it would give her a few mental moments to herself. As she'd expected, he was glad to do so. *Perhaps he is already getting into the Wanderlust groove*, she thought, as he hopped to the front of the group and enthusiastically motioned for them to follow.

As soon as they were seated, Lana excused herself and called Salvatore Romano. His professional tone and his promise to get in touch with Alex straight away were an enormous relief. They agreed to meet up at the hotel in the evening, where he would bring her up to date on the police's case against her boyfriend.

When Lana rejoined her group, she noticed a spring to her step that had been missing since Alex knocked on her hotel room door last night, covered in blood. Her brief conversation with the lawyer gave Lana hope that this nightmare would soon come to an end. Then, and only then, would she allow herself to think about their future together.

To her delight, their meal was already on the table. Romano had sounded so confident that she felt her appetite returning.

The restaurant Dotty had chosen for them was famous for its *risi e bisi*, a dish made from rice and fresh garden peas, and *bigoli in salsa*, a pasta mixed with sardines. The simple dishes were filling and delicious. *Bussolai* biscuits, treats made on the island of Burano, completed the meal.

After she and Tom ordered a last round of drinks for the group, Lana's thoughts turned again to Alex's predicament. Who else could have murdered Matteo? From what she had heard during the police's interrogations, Vittoria, Bianca, Dave, Harry, and George were all in the vicinity of Matteo's office when the cleaner found Alex inside of his office. *Was Chrissy also upstairs at the time of the murder?* she wondered. The police detective almost insinuated that she was. If she had, had George found her in Matteo's office?

Carmen and Rhonda's remarks about the police's interest in Chrissy—implying that she had been in the office—certainly made sense. When she noticed the seat next to George was empty, Lana saw her chance to find out more about his conversation with the police and his wife's whereabouts that night. "Hi, George. Will Chrissy be joining us later?"

"No, she wanted to do her own thing today," George said gruffly before turning away from her.

"Does her not being here have anything to do with the fight you had with Matteo?"

"What of it? You were there—you saw how Matteo got handsy with my wife. I've been one of his most loyal investors and that's how he treats me?" George blew out his cheeks. "If you were in a relationship, you would understand."

Lana sucked back the tears his words almost caused to flow. "I am," she said quietly, realizing he had still not explained why his wife was not by his side, "and I understand how humiliating that must have been. Had she met Matteo before? She did mention something about Seattle."

George whipped around and glared at her. "I already answered the police's questions." He pushed his hefty frame up out of his chair. "Where's the bathroom in this place?"

Lana pointed to the back, and George waddled away without another word.

As she watched him, Lana vowed to talk to Chrissy as soon as possible. Matteo had been the aggressor last night, and Chrissy had clearly rejected his advances. So why did George seem to be mad at his wife, and why would she avoid the group today? *It doesn't make sense*, Lana thought. Unless, she had gone back up to Matteo's office, and George had found her there.

Here we go again, Lana thought. She had hoped that once Randy retired, she would no longer have to worry about having murderers amongst her group. But here she was, again feeling the need to investigate those she was leading around Venice.

She covered her face with her hands, feeling momentarily overwhelmed. *Get it together*, she told herself. The last thing she wanted to do was have her clients to think that she was having a mini-breakdown. And if one of them was a murderer, it was imperative they not know she and Alex were involved. Otherwise they would be on their guard when Lana was present.

Lana excused herself again and rushed to the women's bathroom to wash off her face and compose herself. She stared in the mirror, saddened by her bloodshot eyes and reddened cheeks. Since she had seen her boyfriend be arrested, she had tried to suppress her emotions, but talking with the lawyer made her feel like there was a real chance Alex would get out of this. That sense of relief, paradoxically, had sent Lana into an emotional tailspin.

I could really use a shoulder to cry on or someone to confide in. What I wouldn't give to talk to Willow, she thought. It wasn't just the time difference that stopped Lana from calling. Willow had a young child at home and worked full-time. She didn't want to burden her with this, as well. Once she was back in Seattle, there would be plenty of time for a heart-to-heart.

Thinking of her best friend made her tear up again, just as the door to the bathroom opened and Carmen entered. Lana almost gave herself whiplash when she tried lowering her head over the sink before her guest could catch sight of her splotchy face.

"Hey, Lana. You were gone so long, I wanted to make sure you were alright. It looks like you are not. Does it have anything to do with your boyfriend being arrested?"

"He's not my boyfriend," Lana mumbled, apparently unconvincingly because Carmen's eyebrows shot up as she smirked at the tour guide.

"How did you know? We did everything we could to hide our relationship," Lana replied. "Are you a psychic? Or a spy?"

Carmen shrugged. "It was a lucky guess that you just confirmed. But I was a bit suspicious of how close you two stood next to each other in Murano, and the way your voice seemed to soften when you talked with him. It didn't help that he seemed too young to have been married thirty years, and he did not know that a hip break takes weeks to heal, not a few days."

When Lana opened her mouth to protest, Carmen talked over her. "What really clinched it for me was how you called out his real name and burst into tears when he was arrested. That was unusual, considering he was supposedly a married man who had just joined the tour."

"Alright, I give up. We've been together a little over a year. I can't believe it was that obvious we were a couple," Lana said, choking back a tear.

"Honestly, I don't think the others have noticed. I guess I'm more observant than most. If you need someone to talk to, I'm a pretty good listener. Rhonda, not so much, at least, unless it involves an antique or collectible."

Carmen's simple act of kindness released a tidal wave of emotions. As her tears flowed unhindered, Lana found herself telling her client everything.

"What am I doing?" Lana moaned when she suddenly realized what she had done. It was as if she had been reliving the past few hours' events in a trance. "This is so unprofessional. I shouldn't have burdened you with my troubles. You're on vacation!"

Carmen lightly patted her back. "There, there. Don't worry. I'm quite good at keeping secrets. I won't tell the rest. In fact, I'll keep my ears open for you."

"No! Please don't get involved with this. If one of our group is a killer, I won't be able to protect you."

Carmen smiled mysteriously. "Don't you worry about that. I can take care of myself."

Lana studied Carmen's face as she considered her guest's offer. As nice as it would be to have someone on her side, she was a client. And if Dotty was right, and Matteo had upset Mafia types, Lana could not risk getting her involved in something that was potentially dangerous.

"Look, I know you teach self-defense classes, but this is more serious. The Mafia might be involved," Lana added with a whisper, despite the fact that they were alone in the bathroom. "I cannot let you get tangled up in this. It's way too risky."

Her guest laughed and waved away her concern. "Don't worry—I'm on vacation, remember? I'm not going to get involved in anything dangerous. I don't have the right type of travel insurance for that kind of nonsense."

27

On the Sidelines

When they returned to the group, Lana was glad that the conversation was centered around the grand palazzos and their upcoming excursions, not Alex. Their plates had been cleared, and everyone had a glass of wine in front of them. Lana was touched to see that Tom had ordered one for her, as well.

"Lana, there you are!" Rhonda waved to her as they approached the table. "I finally figured out what I want to do with our free time tomorrow. I would love to see some antique stores. Can you arrange that?"

"I would be delighted to do so. In fact, would you mind if I tagged along?"

Rhonda clapped her hands together. "You mean, like a private tour? Yes, please! If you can sneak away from your other duties, of course."

"We guides also have a free afternoon, and snuffling around in an antique shop sounds like fun."

The rest of the meal flew by, and soon she and Tom were leading their group back to the hotel. All she could think about was her upcoming meeting with the lawyer and what he was finding out from her boyfriend and the police, yet Lana knew there was still work to be done.

She and Tom split the list of dinner and show requests in two, before approaching different receptionists to help them make their guests' wishes come true. Fortunately for them, almost all of the shows playing in town could be booked via a hotel, which saved both guides the trouble of having to visit several ticket offices or trying book tickets by phone.

Carmen and Rhonda were off to the opera, George to his romantic restaurant, and the Windsor crew wanted to see a performance of Vivaldi—at Harry's request. *He really is a man of many contrasts,* Lana thought.

Working together, they were able to secure tickets and reservations to everything rather quickly. After delivering the necessary information to each of their guests, they wished each other well and went their separate ways.

Lana bided her time waiting for the lawyer to call by searching online for information about her guests. Unfortunately, they seemed to have been telling the truth about themselves and their connections to Matteo, and she did not find out anything new.

At precisely six o'clock, the receptionist rang to let her know her guest was in the lobby. Lana skipped downstairs, eager to find out what Alex's new lawyer had learned.

A tall, attractive man greeted her warmly. Something about his welcoming smile made her feel immediately at ease.

"Lana Hansen, it's unfortunate that we meet under these circumstances," Salvatore Romano said. "We have much to discuss. Why don't we talk over there?"

Lana's back grew tense when she noticed he pointed to the same chairs the detective had asked them to sit in, only a few hours ago. "Do you mind if we sit there?" She pointed to the opposite side of the lobby.

If he was perplexed, he didn't show it. Instead, he nodded and followed her over to two wingback chairs.

"Let me first assure you that after speaking with Alex, I do believe he is innocent."

"That's good to know, considering you're his lawyer," she snapped, feeling immediately bad for overreacting. "Sorry, it's just that the stress is really getting to me. How is he? Does he look alright?"

It had only been a few hours, but it felt like months since she had seen her boyfriend last.

"He's alright, but he is concerned. As he should be."

Lana's throat constricted. "What do you mean?"

"The police are investigating several individuals that were in the vicinity of the victim at the time of his death. However, the protesters are the prime suspects. The lead detective is becoming convinced that Matteo surprised Alex and his fellow Earth Warriors, and that someone in their group overreacted and accidentally killed him."

Lana opened her mouth to protest when Romano added, "This isn't the first time that Matteo was targeted by the Earth Warriors. They are working under the assumption that the protest got out of hand, that it was an accident. But because no one is talking, it is impossible for them to move forward. The police have arrested five other members, yet all refuse to speak. I am afraid their silence is being interpreted as a sign of guilt."

"This can't be happening!" she cried. "Alex wasn't the only one the cleaner saw up on the top floor. Not only were three of my guests spotted up there, but the vice president also admitted to being up on the floor when his body was found. She lost out on a major promotion when Matteo announced he was not retiring, only to be named acting CEO after he was found dead."

"That is true, which is why my investigator is looking into her background and the details around her promotion, as we speak," the lawyer responded patiently. "However, neither she nor your guests were found inside Matteo's office, standing over the body."

When Lana crumpled into her chair, Romano added, "Don't worry, I am on your side. But I need you to realize how bad this looks for your boyfriend. I believe that Matteo was dead when Alex found him, but we need to convince the police of that. And that is going to be a tough sell, at least until we find another plausible motive. Which is why my investigator will focus on other suspects—three of whom are in your tour group. Do you have any clues, leads, or suspicious things to report that might help us get started?"

Before she could answer, he raised a finger and added, "To be clear, your employer did warn me that you like to investigate, which is why I promised her that I would make sure you stayed on the sidelines."

"'Like' is a strong word," Lana interjected.

"And I know that Alex is your boyfriend, but I need you to allow me and my investigator handle this. Let me assure you, he is one of the best in Venice."

"I promise," she said solemnly. "As long as you promise to keep me in the loop."

The lawyer must have noticed the steely resolution in her eyes because he smiled as he held out his hand. "It's a deal."

Lana took his hand, feeling more confident that Alex had a chance of getting out of this mess, thanks to the professional team on his side.

"Now, do you have anything else to share with me that you deem useful to this investigation?" He held his pen at the ready and looked up at Lana questioningly.

"Gosh, well, Dave and Kathy Windsor were pretty upset that Matteo had essentially cancelled their contract without telling them. Kathy did say something about them going bankrupt if Matteo didn't pay up. And right before I left the party, I heard them talking to their competitor. When he made clear that he had already signed a contract with Sail Away Cruises, they were all visibly angry, and Dave and Harry stormed off to confront Matteo about it."

"Excellent," he murmured as he jotted the information down.

"And George Fretwell wanted to pull out all the money he had invested in Sail Away Cruises," Lana continued, warming up to the possibilities that one of her guests may have murdered Matteo. "He said it was because he didn't trust Matteo, which is odd considering he had been singing his praises up until Matteo hit on his wife at the party."

"Did you see Matteo making advances towards Chrissy? And did you see how she reacted?"

"Yes, to both. When Matteo put his hand on Chrissy's bottom, she flipped out and threw a drink in his face."

"So his advances were unwanted."

"You could say that, at least based on her physical reaction. Although Matteo did say something about Chrissy not being so cold in Seattle, implying she had been more receptive the last time they met."

"And how did her husband react?"

"He pushed Matteo away from his wife, and they had a verbal blowup.

When Matteo walked away, he made a snide remark about how he would be waiting for Chrissy in his office. That's when George went ballistic."

"I see." The detective was bent over, scribbling furiously in his notebook.

"After Matteo went up to his office to wait for her, George was furious. Chrissy and Vittoria tried to stop him, but he pushed past them and went upstairs to confront Matteo. That's the last time I saw George before I left."

"And how did his wife react?"

"After George stormed off, Chrissy said she wanted to leave. I left her by the bar so I could tell Tom, my fellow guide, that I was escorting her back to the hotel. But when I went back to fetch her, she had disappeared."

"Do you think she went up to Matteo's office?"

"At the time, I did not. I figured she had left the party and taken a water taxi back to the hotel. But now, I'm not so sure."

"Interesting." The lawyer jotted down several more notations.

Lana snuck a peek, but he was writing in Italian.

"I will have my investigator look into Dave and Kathy Windsor, as well as George and Chrissy Fretwell. If you hear or see anything else that could be useful, please let me know. You have my number. But don't forget the promise I made to your boss."

"There may be one more suspect, but he's not a member of my tour group."

The lawyer cocked his head at her.

"What about the museum representative? The gondola statue was stolen that night, and if the newspapers are to be believed, it is worth quite a bit," Lana blurted. She knew that she was grasping at straws, but if it was a robbery, Alex might be less of a suspect.

"Do you mean the statue of a gondola that Matteo showed off during his speech?" the lawyer asked.

"Yes, I'm surprised the police aren't making a bigger deal about it being gone. One of my tour group members is an antiques dealer and said it was worth a small fortune. Not only because of the silversmith who made it, but because it is covered in thousands of dollars in precious stones. Are the police looking for the gondola?"

"I will ask the lead detective about it, but why do you believe its theft has anything to do with Matteo's murder?"

"Because it was meant to be donated to the museum that night, but Matteo changed his mind and had not told the museum representative. They had a nasty fight about it after Matteo's speech, during which he told him to expect a call from the museum's lawyers. Then he was really rude to my clients when they were waiting for a taxi."

Lana noted that he had trouble suppressing a smile. "You think he killed Matteo because he was rude?"

"No," she said, flustered, "not exactly. But he was really upset about how things ended up. What if he left the party, but came back later to steal it? If Matteo caught him in the act, he may have overreacted and hit him."

"Just as the protesters could have, in your opinion."

"I'm just saying that whoever killed Matteo, may not have meant to."

"I agree," he replied and cringed slightly, as if he did not wish to be the bearer of bad news. "However, it would have been incredibly foolish for the museum representative to steal the object, considering his employer would never be able to display it."

Lana blushed when she realized he was correct. "I didn't think of that."

"And several witness statements mention that Matteo asked Vittoria Russo to return it to his office safe. If she had done so, which she claims that she did in her statement, then how did the museum representative get it out of the safe?" the lawyer reasoned.

Lana shrugged. "I don't know."

"Is that all you have for now?" he asked.

"Yes." She didn't know whether what she had shared was important enough to help solve the case, but anything she could do to help Alex was a step in the right direction. It would take a miracle to get his name cleared before her tour was over, but Lana prayed that this lawyer and his investigator were capable of performing them.

"This is exactly the sort of information you can help me gather," he said with a smile. "But please don't forget our agreement. We'll do the investigating."

Lana felt as if a weight had been lifted off her shoulders. "And you'll keep me in the loop. I'll get in touch, as soon as I hear anything else of interest."

28

Ships Passing in the Night

After her talk with Salvatore Romano, Lana felt as if there was real hope that Alex would get out of this. But it also reminded Lana that she still hadn't seen Chrissy since late last night.

When she inquired about her whereabouts at the hotel reception desk, the clerk nodded. "She just got back from the day spa. I believe I see her sitting at the bar."

Lana followed the woman's finger until she spotted her guest perched on a barstool. "Thanks."

To Lana's relief, Chrissy looked healthy and happy. Her revealing dress made it easy for Lana to search her face and body for bruises.

Chrissy eyed Lana critically. "Why are you checking me out?"

"I'm sorry," Lana stammered. "George was so incensed, I was worried he might have lashed out and hurt you."

Chrissy patted Lana's hand. "That is so sweet. We women have to watch out for each other. But don't you worry, honey. If George even tried to hit me, that would be the end of him. I would take him to court and wring every last penny out of him."

She smiled humorlessly. "Now what can I do for you? Would you join me for a drink?"

Lana shook her head. "It's alright, I didn't want to disturb you. When you didn't join the tour this morning, I was concerned. Especially when George said you didn't want to come to Murano."

"You saw through his lies, too—good for you."

"Chrissy, I have to ask. At the end of the masquerade ball, you said you wanted to leave. But after I talked to Tom, I couldn't find you anywhere. Where did you go?"

Chrissy grimaced. "I went to a cocktail bar on Saint Mark's Square and foolishly had a few more. Not that I needed them, but after that tiff with Matteo, I wanted to clear my head. When I got back to the hotel, the police were searching our floor. I let them check my room, then I took a hot bath and went to bed."

That explained why she hadn't seen Chrissy in the hallway, after the police knocked on everyone's doors. "When did George get back to the hotel?"

"About an hour later. He was so worked up about Matteo's death, the break-in, and being questioned by the police that he woke me up."

"But why is George mad at you?" Lana blurted out. "Matteo was flirting with you, not the other way around."

Chrissy's eyes darkened. "That's personal and irrelevant. Trust me, it's not worth killing over."

Lana could feel her frustration boiling over. If their fight had anything to do with Matteo's death, she needed to know. Especially if it was because Chrissy had gone back up to Matteo's office. Their argument may be the key to finding out what really happened to him that night.

She leaned in close to Chrissy. "Let me tell you something personal and relevant—the man the police arrested for murdering Matteo is my boyfriend, Alex. He was upstairs, taking part in that Earth Warriors protest, but he didn't kill anyone. Unfortunately, he did find the body, which is when the cleaner discovered him inside of Matteo's office. I just met with Alex's lawyer, and he told me the police seem to be certain that Alex is involved—which he is not!"

Lana wrung her hands and locked eyes with Chrissy. "I am asking you, woman to woman: did you go up to Matteo's office, and did George find you there? Is that what your fight was about?"

Chrissy stared at her for a long time before finally breaking eye contact to finish her drink. Only after she had signaled the bartender for two more did she answer. "No, I did not go up to Matteo's office. It was only after George got back to the hotel and we talked things out that he had reason to be mad at me."

When Chrissy grew quiet, Lana pushed, "Pretty much everyone at the party heard Matteo say something about you and Seattle. Did you two have an affair?"

Chrissy snorted. "'Affair' is a strong word. It was more of a one-night stand." She pushed one glass over to Lana before raising her drink and nodding at Lana to do the same.

When their glasses met in the air, Chrissy mumbled, "Cheers," before drinking a significant portion of her Aperol spritz. Lana took a tiny sip of the strong concoction, then let it rest on the bar.

"That remark about Seattle was all George needed to put the pieces together. As soon as he got back to the hotel, he started grilling me about it. It was two years ago, and Matteo was dead—yet George had to keep pushing! So I finally told him the truth, that I had slept with Matteo when he flew over to Seattle to meet with George's investment firm."

Lana swallowed hard. "Oh, I see. If it was a one-time thing, then I take it you two weren't really in love?"

Chrissy's laugh was as bitter as their drink. "Heavens, no! Matteo was quite flirtatious, and I was looking to get revenge on George. You see, my darling husband had slept with his assistant while they were attending a conference. Common, isn't it? I only found out about his fling because I found their messages on his phone. That was a day or so before Matteo arrived. His timing was perfect, otherwise I wouldn't have given him the time of day."

Lana had to scoop her jaw off the bar. Chrissy said it so casually, as if cheating on one's spouse was an everyday occurrence.

"I don't know why I didn't get out of town for the weekend so I could clear my head, instead of accompanying George to that dinner. Looking back, that would have been the better course of action. But I was in denial that my husband would do something like that to me."

Chrissy paused to take another swig of her drink, emptying half the glass in the process. "We had already made dinner reservations at the Seattle Space Needle for the night Matteo arrived. George wanted to impress him, and the views from up there always work—at least, if it's not raining. But that night, Seattle was in full glory, and we all had too much to drink and eat. By the end of the night, George could barely stand up. It was embarrassing, to say the least."

Chrissy lowered her voice, apparently embarrassed by what she was about to share next. "Matteo had to help me get him into a taxi. After we got home and Matteo helped me get George into bed, he put his hand on my back to comfort me. Something about that simple gesture just released something wild in me. When I turned to him and he kissed me, I just let myself get lost in the moment. Unfortunately, that moment didn't last long, and afterwards, I felt horrible about cheating on my husband. Getting revenge in that way didn't bring the sense of relief I had hoped it would."

Lana couldn't stop squirming in her chair. *Is this how priests feel after hearing a confession involving sexual promiscuity?* she wondered. After leading so many tours, she had gotten used to guests opening up to her and sometimes sharing secrets they had never told another soul. But she still had not gotten used to how uncomfortable these sorts of intimate confessions made her feel.

"That's why I didn't join George last year, when he flew over for Matteo's party," Chrissy continued, apparently unaware of Lana's distress. "I didn't want to see him. But this year, George surprised me with a weeklong trip to Paris before we flew over to Venice so we could go to that stupid party. I couldn't have said no to the trip without it looking suspicious. I thought Matteo would have enough decorum not to mention our brief encounter. Sadly, I was wrong. But then, Matteo had way too much to drink and was saying all sorts of things he should not have."

"What are you going to do now? Stay in Venice, or fly home?"

Chrissy stared off into the distance. "I know it sounds crazy, but I am going to stay here and try to save my marriage."

"I don't know if it's my place to say, but George did ask us to book a romantic restaurant for you two, tonight. So it sounds like he's open to trying."

Chrissy's smile was manic. "He better be. He was the one who started this when he slept with his assistant. Despite his actions, I still love that old fool, and I know that deep down, he still loves me, too. He's the father to my children and has always been a devoted companion. It's too bad he couldn't keep his pants on at that conference, but I would rather forgive him than not be with him."

When she noticed Lana's shocked expression, she picked up her drink and added, "It took a lot of therapy to get here, trust me. If we didn't have kids, I may not have bothered to try."

"Chrissy, I appreciate your candor. I need you to be honest with me once again—do you think George killed Matteo?"

"Over me?" Chrissy laughed heartily, until a wave of concern washed over her face. "I don't think so. He didn't know that we had actually slept together—at least I hadn't told him. But I don't know if he talked to Matteo after I left or not."

"And if Matteo told him about you two..." Lana let her voice trail off, leaving the question open.

"No." Chrissy shook her head resolutely. "He wouldn't have. George's ego was bruised only because Matteo humiliated him publicly. But it wasn't the first time someone embarrassed him in public, and he's never killed anyone before."

Lana squeezed her hands and rose. "Thank you."

Chrissy pulled her back onto the barstool. "You don't think George did it, do you?"

Lana shrugged her shoulders. "I wish I knew. I hope you'll consider returning to the tour."

Chrissy nodded and picked up her drink. She stared at the half-filled glass before setting it back down on the bar. "Do you know where George is?"

"Last I saw him, he was heading up to your hotel room."

"I think it's time to have another heart-to-heart with my husband. We are in the world's most romantic city. It's a shame to waste our time here fighting."

Lana nodded, wondering whether that was the real reason. Or whether her questions had got Chrissy thinking more about that night.

Her client laid a hand on Lana's shoulder. "Thanks for the girl talk. I needed that."

When Chrissy walked off, presumably to find her husband, Lana stayed to finish her drink. Her client's words about forgiving and forgetting sometimes being the only way forward reverberated in her mind.

Their talk helped Lana to see Alex's actions in another light. *Chrissy is right. I've made it clear that I was mad and hurt, but now we have to find a way to move forward*, she thought. *As soon as I figure out how to get him out of jail.*

29

Twofaced Liar

April 24—Day Six of the Wanderlust Tour in Venice, Italy

When Lana entered the breakfast hall, the large group of tourists clustered around the television set caught her attention. Since the manhunt began, it had been set to BBC News so their international guests could keep up to date. Lana could imagine the hotel staff was overwhelmed with questions and concerns since Alex had been arrested outside of their entrance.

She was happy to see that her guests had not yet arrived because it gave her time to take in the news segment that had the small crowd abuzz.

The BBC announcer was relaying new information about the prime suspect in Matteo Conti's murder—according to the presenter, a dedicated Earth Warriors activist. Her stomach clenched as she watched the montage of grainy video footage and security cameras showing snippets of several actions their suspect had taken part in. Her boyfriend's face had been circled in red, so the viewer could identify him more easily. Lana watched in horror as Alex illegally boarded a fishing trawler, waved the flag of the Earth Warriors from the deck of a ship blocking oil tankers, rappelled off the roof of a clothing factory known for using child labor, and hung off the Tyne Bridge with a sign in his hand protesting whale fishing.

While the images played, the presenter explained to his viewers which protest actions they were watching and the cities in which they had taken place. According to the news reader, the police had identified Alex as having taken part in six protests during the past four months.

"That twofaced liar!" Lana hissed through her teeth. Alex wasn't on the periphery, but smack dab in the middle of the action. Who was this person? The Alex Wright she knew and loved would never have taken part in something illegal.

"Can you believe I had lunch with a killer?" George said, his voice close behind her.

"It is incredible to think you spent the day with him," his wife replied.

Lana wiped away the angry tears that had just sprung up, then turned to her guests, surprised to see the Fretwells standing behind her holding hands, as if nothing bad had happened between them.

Chrissy smiled at Lana and winked. "That restaurant you recommended was perfect."

"He was so quiet," Harry added, his eyes glued to the television screen. "Yet from the looks of it, he must be quite a crazy guy."

"Lana, did you ever figure out how that maniac weaseled his way onto our tour?" Dave asked.

She bit her tongue, knowing she had to continue pretending that she did not know Alex. Before Lana could respond, Carmen said, "I bet it was someone on Matteo's staff, not that environmentalist, who did him in. It sure sounds like he was difficult to work with."

"You can say that again," George chimed in.

Lana smiled slyly at Carmen, who nodded slightly.

When the news segment ended, her guests turned to the breakfast buffet and filled up their plates. After a long breakfast, during which the news footage dominated the conversation, the two guides got their group back outside.

"So, folks," Tom said, a grin splitting his face, "we have a treat for the art lovers today. Our first stop is the Peggy Guggenheim Collection, followed by a guided walk through the surrounding neighborhood, famous for its many contemporary art galleries. And last, a lovely lunch on the water before your free afternoon begins."

Their walk took them back over the Accademia Bridge and through the Dorsoduro district. They followed Tom past fairy-tale palazzos and grand churches. The residential neighborhood was full of colorful, crumbling mansions, dainty staircases over thin waterways, and open squares filled with tourists and locals dining. Gondolas and speedboats played peekaboo with them as they crisscrossed over hidden walkways and Escher-like bridges.

Several buildings on the street were tall, majestic structures with latticed stone worked into the fronts and backs. Most had apartments above and shops below, the majority occupied by expensive art galleries, jewelers, and glass shops. Lana noticed those on their left butted up against the Grand Canal. Through tiny alleyways and gates, she could see most had a pier extending out the back with boats worth millions seemingly tied up to them with a simple rope.

A glorious gate made of wire and glass beads marked the entrance to the Peggy Guggenheim Collection. Their group was ushered past the long line and into the garden that also served as the entrance to the museum. A guide was waiting to take them on a brief tour through the collection, before they had a little bit of free time to explore the space at their own pace.

Lana paused to read a few of the messages hanging in Yoko Ono's *Magic Wish Tree*, before following their guide inside. As much as she wanted to double back and leave her own wish, "seeing your boyfriend get released from jail" was on a whole different level than the hopes for world peace and an end to hunger that the majority of visitors had tied to the olive branches.

Peggy Guggenheim's former home on the Grand Canal had been turned into a palace for her exquisite modern art collection. Peggy, the niece of Solomon R. Guggenheim, had been alive and buying at the right moment for the type of cubist, abstract, and surrealist art that she loved.

Not only was her collection of modern art one of the finest in Europe, the lady herself sounded like a wonderful maverick, feminist, and all-around interesting person. *What I wouldn't give to have attended one of her wild parties,* Lana thought, as she listened to their guide describe the museum's namesake and her many famous friends.

Their guide walked faster than Lana would have liked through the many small rooms, each dedicated to a different artist, period, or theme. She marveled at the masterworks by Constantin Brâncuși, Georges Braque, Salvador Dali, Joan Miró, René Magritte, Jean Arp, and more. Thanks to her job, she had visited many of Europe's most important museums. This was, hands down, one of the most interesting modern art collections she had ever seen.

During their tour, Lana spotted a mobile—a piece of moving artwork—created by Alexander Calder, an artist she loved. She had seen several of his works in other museums, but never one made of anything other than metal before.

According to the sign, it was the only Calder mobile displayed in a public museum that was made from wood, string, and metal. The rawness of the material added an edge to his work that spoke to her. The shapes and their positioning reminded her of the solar system, with moons, stars, and planets rotating around the sun. It was fascinating.

By the time the tour ended, Lana's head was spinning as her brain tried processing all the beautiful artwork they had seen.

After the guide walked off to meet his next group, her clients split up for a half hour to explore the museum on their own. The Windsor crew stepped out onto the magnificent balcony at the back of the building, George and Chrissy skipped over to the museum's café, while Rhonda and Carmen turned back towards the artwork.

She watched through the window as the Windsors scored seats on the dock stretching along the back of the museum, and settled back into the sun. Kathy's earlier remark about Windsor Custom Watercraft going bankrupt if Matteo didn't pay his outstanding bill reverberated in her head. Now that he was dead, it seemed to Lana that they had even less chance at getting Sail Away Cruises to pay the bill. What would be the impact on their company's future? Seeing the Windsors outside, away from the others, made Lana realize that now was the perfect time to find out.

When Lana stepped outside, she had to pause and take in the incredible views. They had seen the same sights up on the Accademia Bridge, but the dock was placed so low on the Grand Canal that you seemed to be at eye level with the gondoliers. Lana understood why Peggy Guggenheim had wanted to live here—it was truly magical.

Dave and Kathy waved at Lana when she stepped outside. *That was easy,* she thought, and sauntered over to them. The large dock extended far into the Grand Canal, and its surface was dotted with large benches. Two poles painted blue and yellow were planted in the water just before the dock, contrasting nicely with the building's white exterior.

Uncertain how to begin, Lana dove in, headfirst. "I hope you two are doing alright today."

When Kathy and Dave looked up at her, a perplexed expression on their faces, she added, "It is too bad about Sail Away not purchasing your fleet. I hope that hasn't ruined your trip."

Their confusion was immediately replaced with joy. "Actually, they are going to buy the ships, after all. Vittoria called us yesterday evening to let us know that the board approved the final payment for the fleet we already built for Matteo. And she even inquired about us building another ten ships for them. Can you believe it? It all worked out," Kathy said, the relief in her voice evident.

"That's fantastic news! Now you don't have to worry about going bankrupt."

Dave looked stricken, but Kathy waved her comment away. "I was upset when I said that. We are financially solid enough that we wouldn't have gone belly up if Sail Away hadn't paid us what they owed us. And we would have found a buyer for their ships, eventually."

She sure has changed her tune, Lana thought.

Before she could continue, Tom popped out onto the dock. "Wow, what a view. Hey, guys, the guide for our walking tour is waiting for us by the outside gate. Is everyone ready to go?"

Lana and her guests rose and followed Tom inside. As she watched Dave and Kathy, holding hands and smiling, she couldn't help but think how convenient it was for the Windsors that Vittoria was now the acting CEO.

30

Proving Your Worth

Tom led them through a maze of picturesque streets towards their lunch destination. The restaurant was located in a large square enclosed by two churches and many salmon-colored buildings. Half of the storefronts were cafés and restaurants, their tables placed far into the square. In the open center, street musicians played accordion while children chased the many pigeons and seagulls, on the hunt for leftovers. Coming across such a large space was a breath of fresh air in this congested part of Venice.

Before they could find the correct café, George stopped and stared. "Well, I'll be. The rumors must be true."

When he began to grow red in the face, Chrissy grabbed his hand. "What's wrong?"

"Vittoria is playing me, just like Matteo did! That's the owner of Sail Away Cruises' biggest competitor." He nodded towards a table in the center of a terrace they had just passed, where Vittoria was sitting with a sharply dressed older man.

"Rumor has it, they offered Vittoria their CEO position a few months ago, but Sail Away's board had already promised her Matteo's spot, as soon as he retired. She told me she was staying, but maybe she found something about Sail Away's finances that I do not know and is thinking of jumping ship."

He turned to his wife. "I'm sorry, my pet, but I need to know if she lied to me, before I sign over any more money."

159

After Chrissy nodded in assent, he strode over to Vittoria. Before he could reach their table, she noticed his approach and sprung up, holding out one hand as if to stop him. She said something to her table companion, then wove her way past George and back into the open square.

George followed, his anger growing by the second. "What's going on? Yesterday you assured me that you were going to stay and lead Sail Away Cruises. That's the only reason why I didn't pull all of my money out of the company. So what are you doing talking with him?"

"Trust me, I am going to accept the board's offer and stay on as CEO. There is only one hitch—their initial offer is for twenty percent less than what they were paying Matteo. It's devilish of me, I know, but I think they should match his salary. Which is why I told them that I was going to take this meeting."

"How did they respond?"

"They panicked. No one else is ready or able to step in to fill Matteo's shoes. And with his sudden death, the company needs a strong leader to take control, if only to reassure the stockholders. But I sensed they didn't believe I would follow through with my threat, which is why I chose this spot for our meeting. Sail Away's board of directors has a monthly luncheon at the restaurant next door." Vittoria glanced at her watch, and her eyes twinkled. "In fact, they should be here any minute. I suspect they will be even more nervous if they see you here with me. You are one of Sail Away Cruises' biggest investors, after all."

When George hesitated, Vittoria murmured, "I'll make it worth your while. A higher percentage of return on your new investments, perhaps?"

Lana swore she could see George's eyes turning green, just thinking about all that money. *Vittoria is going to make a great CEO,* Lana thought, *she's certainly intelligent and cutthroat enough to succeed.*

George smiled. "It's a deal. I look forward to having you at the helm." He turned towards the rest. "If you don't mind, Lana, Chrissy and I are going to join Vittoria for a drink. We'll be over in a few minutes."

"Of course, good luck."

When Lana began to walk away, Dave stepped forward. "Hi, Vittoria, it was good to talk with you yesterday."

Distracted by George's interruption, Vittoria apparently hadn't seen the Windsors standing close by. Her face lit up, and she walked over to shake the couple's hands.

"It was wonderful speaking to you two, as well. I look forward to working with your company for many years to come. In fact, if you have time this afternoon, perhaps we can hammer out the details of our next contract?"

"We will make time," Dave said firmly. "Why don't we come over to your office after we are done here—say, in two hours?"

"Excellent. I will have my assistant chill a bottle of champagne for us, to celebrate." Vittoria looked to her table companion, now intently studying Lana's tour group. "If you will excuse me, I should get back. I will see you two later. George, Chrissy, would you join me?"

She sauntered back to her table, with the Fretwells in tow.

"What a lady," Dave said. "She is going to make a great CEO."

"She certainly has the drive and smarts to do it," Kathy agreed. "It really is a blessing that Matteo is gone, isn't it?"

Dave began to nod in agreement, but stopped when he noticed Lana watching them. "Which restaurant is ours?" he said.

"It's the next one on the left," Tom answered. "Come on, gang, it looks like they have a few free tables left under the parasols."

"That's good to hear," Rhonda said. "I feel like I'm wilting in this hot sun. It is nice to get a tan, though."

"I hadn't expected to have to wear sunscreen in April," Carmen agreed.

Lana waited for her group to pass before picking up the rear. *Vittoria again*, she thought. She sure seemed to be a key player in this mess and had certainly gotten what she wanted since Matteo was murdered. And now—thanks to her—George and the Windsors were getting what they wanted, as well.

Lana briefly thought of Agatha Christie's *Murder on the Orient Express*, wondering if the four of them could have worked together to kill Matteo Conti. *This isn't fiction, but real life*, she chastised herself. The chances of that happening were pretty much nil.

While waiting for her clients to get seated, Lana glanced over at Vittoria's table again. As she watched the acting CEO chatting animatedly with her three tablemates, Lana couldn't help but wonder what dark secrets or hidden skeletons Romano's investigator would uncover in her closet.

31

Exchanging Information

When they returned to the hotel after another delicious lunch, Lana spotted Alex's lawyer sitting in the lobby. When they made eye contact, she held up a finger, letting him know that she would be right over.

After she and Tom checked that their guests had all of the information they needed for their free afternoon, she waved goodbye to the Fretwells, the Windsor crew, and her fellow guide, before turning to Carmen and Rhonda.

"Would you mind if we left in about five minutes? I need to talk to that man over there. As soon as I'm done, we can go to the antiques shops."

"Take your time. I'm going to treat Rhonda to a prosecco," Carmen declared.

"So early in the day?" Rhonda tittered, then shrugged. "Why not, we are on vacation."

As Carmen passed by, she whispered to Lana, "Is that your boyfriend's lawyer?"

"Yes, it is," she whispered back.

Carmen lightly squeezed her shoulder, then steered her friend towards the hotel bar.

Lana sat down in the chair across from Salvatore Romano. "I was just about to call you with some new information."

"Excellent," the lawyer smiled. "I have new information for you, as well. My investigator has been quite busy."

"Why don't you go first?" Lana offered.

"Alright. For us, the biggest revelation is that Matteo was under investigation for fraud."

"What did he do?"

"Matteo had convinced several business associates to invest in bitcoins, but it was a scam and he pocketed the money, instead."

Lana cringed. "Ouch."

"The lawsuit was directed at him, but it would have reflected back on the company. I can imagine it would have negatively affected Sail Away's stock prices and tarnished its reputation to the point that it may have bankrupted the company. We know your tour guest, George Fretwell, is a major investor in Sail Away. We have found no proof that he knew about the fraud investigation, but I do wonder: has he mentioned it?"

"No, and in fact, he is keeping his money in Sail Away and possibly investing more into the company. We just ran into Vittoria—the acting CEO—and I heard them discussing it."

The lawyer tapped his chin. "Interesting. If the case against Matteo had gone to court, it would have cost George a significant amount of his investment. From what my team has uncovered, he's already poured three million dollars into it."

"Oh, my," Lana sputtered. "That explains how he could drop ten grand on a necklace."

Romano squinted up at her, a questioning look in his eye.

Lana blushed. "Never mind—it's not important."

The lawyer looked at his notebook before continuing. "We have also discovered that Windsor Custom Watercraft is on the verge of bankruptcy. Their bank is demanding payment on several overdue loans. From what my investigator has discovered, without that final check from Sail Away Cruises, they would not have survived more than a few weeks."

"What? Kathy said she was exaggerating when she said they would go bankrupt." Lana bit her lip. "Though that doesn't matter now. She just told me that Vittoria already agreed to pay the outstanding invoice and even wants to order more ships from them."

"So both George and the Windsors benefited greatly from Matteo's death. This is useful information," Romano said as he bent over his notebook. "Right now, Alex needs all the help he can get."

"How is he doing?" she whispered.

"He is upset and confused. Most of all, he doesn't understand why the other protesters refuse to back up his story. But there is hope. If we can show that another person had the motive and means to kill Matteo, it might be enough to cast suspicion on someone else and force the police to set Alex free."

Despite his reassurances, Lana didn't feel the same surge of hope she had after their first conversation. Right now, all she felt was dismay.

32

Shopping for Antiques

"That's a Tiffany Linenfold lamp!" Rhonda exclaimed. "I didn't expect to see one of those in here. I sold a similar lamp a few months ago, though mine was in better condition. They usually sell for three to five thousand. But given the tears in the fabric, for this one I would ask, two, maybe two and half."

"You mean thousand, right?" Lana asked.

"Yep." Rhonda looked around for the antique shop's owner. "I'm going to go check and see if I'm right."

She slipped away before Carmen could stop her. "There's a price card right there." She pointed it out to Lana. "And look—Rhonda was right on the money."

Indeed, according to the tiny price tag, the shop was asking two thousand for it.

"That's incredible! Rhonda is quite good at evaluating an object's value."

So far, Rhonda had walked through each of the shops at a snail's pace, intently studying everything they came across. Without even touching the objects, she had valued almost all of them accurately.

Carmen blushed with pride, as if she had taught Rhonda everything she knew. "Some fish, some play soccer, Rhonda guesses prices. It's her sport, which is what makes her shop so successful. I call her the antique whisperer," Carmen said softly before breaking out into a loud guffaw. "Seriously, it is an amazing gift."

"Ladies!" Rhonda skipped back towards them. "I was right about the lamp—they are asking two grand for it. Say, I could use a second opinion. There is the most beautiful pair of vintage earrings over by the register, but they look pricey. Could you tell me what you think of them?"

The antiques dealer led them over to an enclosed display case, in which a necklace and earrings rested on a velvet stand. The necklace was a thick gold band with a large yellow gemstone hanging off of a pendant that reminded Lana of a sunflower. The stone was cut like a diamond and shimmered under the strong spotlights. The earrings consisted of three small yellow sapphires hanging from a leaf-shaped gold stud. The vintage pieces were simple in design, yet elegantly beautiful and unique.

"The stones are yellow sapphire, which is fairly rare in that kind of setting. And I've never seen a pendant that resembles a sunflower before," Rhonda said. "I would value the necklace at five thousand, simply because of the size of that sapphire. But the earrings shouldn't cost more than a thousand. The stones are significantly smaller."

Lana whistled under her breath. The earrings were gorgeous, but she couldn't imagine paying so much for any one piece of jewelry.

Yet Carmen began to nod enthusiastically. "They are perfect for you. That color really suits your skin tone and hair color."

When Rhonda turned to Lana, a questioning look in her eye, she shrugged. "One thousand dollars for a single pair of earrings is out of my league, Rhonda. I think they are gorgeous, but I could never afford to buy them."

Rhonda squeezed her arm and smiled. "That's all I wanted to hear." She rushed off to find the shopkeeper again. Lana watched as she gestured towards the jewelry before she and the owner began negotiating for a price. Based on Rhonda's increasingly agitated movements and frustrated expression, she was not getting the deal she had hoped for.

When she returned a few minutes later, her smile had vanished.

"He wanted double," she huffed. "What a rip-off! I thought a thousand was already on the high side for what they are really worth, but they are unique and I figured they were worth splurging on."

"We are really close to Saint Mark's Square," Lana reasoned. "Maybe they have higher margins because of the fabulous location."

"I suppose that is their tourist price. I bet a local wouldn't have to pay so much." Rhonda pursed her lips and folded her arms over her torso.

Carmen patted her on the back. "Well, my friend, are you going to let this deal ruin the afternoon, or should we check out the next shop?"

"Let's see what the next store brings."

Rhonda's professional pride was soon restored after she managed to negotiate down the price of a lovely silver necklace at the next shop. Once she returned with her purchase, Rhonda patted at her forehead with a tissue.

"What do you two say to a nice glass of iced tea? I could use a short break before we check out the rest of the shops."

"That sounds great; it is hot today. Do you have any suggestions, Lana?"

The two friends exited the shop, Lana at their heels. When she stopped to take her phone out of her bag, her purse's strap caught on something, momentarily pulling her backwards. She threw out her arms to keep her balance. "What was that?"

When she looked around for the source, her eyes fell on Bianca, Matteo's assistant. The young lady was pushing the strap to her backpack up onto her shoulder. "My bag's clasp got tangled up with your purse, I'm afraid."

As she made eye contact with Lana, her expression softened. "Hey—I know you! You're the tour guide, for Wanderlust Tours, right?"

When she nodded, Bianca added, "I just dropped off your invitations to Matteo's funeral. They are waiting for you at your hotel's front desk."

"You what now?" Lana cocked her head, certain she had misheard the young lady.

"Vittoria had already mentioned it to the Fretwells and the Windsors, and both couples seemed enthusiastic about attending."

"Why?" Lana blurted out, slightly disturbed that her guests wanted to attend the funeral of a man they seemed to despise.

Bianca apparently interpreted her question in another manner. "Because you were at the masquerade ball, Vittoria figured you would all want to pay your last respects, so you are all invited." She looked around before leaning in and whispering, "It should be quite the party. The society columns have already called it the funeral of the year—and it's only April!"

Something about Bianca's wicked grin made Lana's stomach tighten. Matteo had been the man of honor at the most anticipated party and funeral of the year. It was a dubious honor, indeed.

"Oh, okay, thanks."

"No problem," Bianca said. She was so much bubblier and happier than she had looked at the masquerade ball. When she began to bounce away, Lana called her back. "How are you holding up? I can imagine Matteo's death was quite a shock."

Bianca's eyes widened. "You can say that. It was a real wakeup call. Life is too short to keep doing what you do not love. I promised Vittoria I would stay long enough to get her assistant up to speed on all of my current projects. After that, I am moving back to my village in Tuscany. I tried living on my own in the big city, but I miss my family and friends."

"What does your family think?"

"My parents are thrilled that I'm moving back home, even if it's only temporary. Since my brother went off to college, they are suffering from empty-nest syndrome."

Lana smiled. "That sounds perfect." Bianca seemed so naïve, she really needed someone to watch over her.

"Bianca—is that you? I hardly recognized you without your ball gown," Carmen teased. She and Rhonda must have noticed that Lana was no longer behind them and doubled back.

"Fancy seeing you here. What are you up to?" Rhonda asked.

"Hello! It's nice to see you both again. Are you enjoying your tours of Venice?" Bianca asked, delight in her voice. Apparently the three had talked during the masquerade ball and had hit it off.

"This is such a gorgeous city—you are so lucky to live here, Bianca. We did have to take a break from our excursions to do some antiques shopping, though," Carmen said.

"That is delightful. You are sure to find many treasures today."

"Are you here to shop, as well?" Rhonda asked.

"No, to sell. I'm getting rid of a few trinkets my grandmother left me, so I don't have to ask my parents for money for the bus ride home. Of course, that depends on how much I can wrangle out of an antiques dealer. They do tend to lowball clients. I'll probably have to visit several shops before I receive a fair price."

"Rhonda owns an antiques shop back in the States. Maybe she could take a look for you, so you know what you should be getting," Carmen offered. "It might help you in your negotiations."

To Lana's surprise, Bianca did not accept the offer with gratitude, but grew pale in the face. "That is generous of you, but I have sold antiques to a few of the local shops before."

"It would be no trouble..." Rhonda added as she reached for the younger woman's backpack.

Bianca jerked her bag away and looked at her watch, grimacing as she read its face. "Gosh, look at the time. I'm going to be late for my date if I don't hurry up. And I really need to take care of this first. I'll see you at the funeral, okay?"

Bianca smiled and waved as she entered the shop, closing the door firmly behind her.

Only after they were a block away did Carmen snap her fingers. "Shoot! I forgot to ask her about the gondola statue."

"I talked to the lawyer about that, and it's a dead end," Lana replied. "Even if that representative stole it, the museum would not be able to display it."

"That's a good point. Oh, well, that's that. Where to now, Lana?"

As she led her guests to the nearest café, Lana could not help but think about the invitations Bianca had left at their hotel. As macabre as it sounded to attend a funeral during their tour, it would give her a chance to see—and possibly speak to—Vittoria again. The acting CEO of Sail Away Cruises seemed have gained the most by Matteo's death, was the last person to have seen the gondola before it was stolen, and was on the top floor around the time of his murder.

The fates had dropped this invitation in her lap—Lana knew she could not pass up this opportunity, despite her promise to Alex's lawyer. *Whatever information I see or hear, I'll pass along to Romano and let his investigator deal with it,* Lana told herself.

But first, she had a more pressing matter. How was she going to convince her guests to attend Matteo's funeral?

33

Exclusive Invitation

April 25—Day Seven of the Wanderlust Tour in Venice, Italy

It turned out that Lana need not have worried. When she mentioned it at breakfast the next morning, her guests were immediately enthusiastic. They had already heard about the funeral as it had been heavily featured on the afternoon and evening news. Apparently many heads of important companies would be attending, and there were even rumors that royals would come to pay their last respects, as well. Her group were thrilled to be invited to this exclusive event.

"That means that we won't be able to attend the opera," Lana said, double-checking that no one would be upset.

"I was looking forward to seeing a performance in the Teatro La Fenice, but this funeral sounds quite special. I would hate to miss it," Carmen said.

Chrissy giggled and leaned in as if she was telling them all a secret. "I read in a British newspaper that the prince and his wife will be attending. I might need a new dress for this. Something semi-transparent, I think. It's too hot to wear all black, otherwise."

George kissed the back of her hand. "I don't think, I know so. Why don't we head out and do some shopping? The funeral doesn't start until noon, right, Lana?"

"That's correct. I guess we are all free to do what we want until then. Why don't we meet back here in the lobby at eleven-thirty and we can take a water taxi over together?"

"Sounds good," George said, as he led his wife towards the exit.

Lana watched them leave, amazed at how easily they had gone back to being lovey-dovey. Was that the secret to a long and happy marriage—the ability to forgive and forget?

If they can get over something as crushing as infidelity, Alex and I should be able to get through this current crisis. All he has to do is tell me the truth about the protests he participated in and then we can move on, Lana thought.

Dave looked to his wife. "We would like to take a walk, as well. It's been one heck of a week, and it would be good to just relax a little before the funeral starts."

"We have been on an emotional roller coaster since we got here, haven't we," Kathy added. "Now that we have received the last payment and signed a new contact with Sail Away Cruises, I finally feel like we are on vacation. But the trip is almost over!"

"Why don't we stay in Europe for another week? I don't know about Venice, but maybe we can catch a train to Rome? I haven't been to the Vatican in years."

Kathy leaned in and kissed her husband, displaying their first act of public affection since this trip began. "I think that's a wonderful idea. But this time, Harry and Joe are not invited."

Dave chuckled as their lips met again.

"I would like to take a gondola ride. I know it's expensive, but Venice is the only place you can really ride one—outside of Las Vegas. But that's not really the same thing," Rhonda said. "Come on, Carmen, it's my treat."

"Francis would not have approved, but your husband would have. Let's do it for Richard," Carmen said, and Rhonda smiled at the mention of her husband's name.

"For Richard," Rhonda repeated. "Why don't you join us, Lana?"

"I do appreciate the offer, but there's only room for two in those heart-shaped seats. You go on and enjoy yourselves. I'd like to sort a few things out before the funeral."

"Alright, good luck," Carmen said.

"What about me?" Tom asked, after all of their clients had left.

"As far as I'm concerned, you are free until eleven-thirty."

A smile split his face. "Excellent. Enjoy your morning."

"Thanks." Lana waited until she was alone before returning to her room to call Salvatore Romano.

Unfortunately, Alex's lawyer was not available, and Lana didn't leave a message. Instead, she sat on her balcony, taking in the sights as she considered who had the most to gain from Matteo Conti's death.

If Matteo was still alive, the Windsors probably would have gone bankrupt, Vittoria would have missed out on a lucrative promotion, and George would have lost a ridiculous amount of money when that fraud investigation went to court.

Since being named acting CEO, Vittoria had already signed contracts to purchase more of the Windsors' ships and had convinced George to invest even more money in the company.

And George, Vittoria, and Dave had all been spotted on the upper floor around the time Matteo's body was found, Lana realized.

She tapped her chin, reflecting on the possibilities. So which one had been angry or desperate enough to commit murder?

34

Funeral of the Year

The funeral of the year was held in Venice's largest church, the Basilica dei Santi Giovanni e Paolo. Lana and her group had visited it on the first day of their tour, but it looked quite different today, decked out with a plethora of floral arrangements and garlands suitable for this formal affair.

She gazed around the church, filled with important and famous guests offering each other condolences, figuring this was what a head of state's funeral would be like.

During the lengthy service, several corporate leaders and minor celebrities shared anecdotes about Matteo, almost all involving a deal they worked on together or a cruise that he convinced them to book. Only one family member—a distant cousin—spoke, and her stories about Matteo were as impersonal as those of his business associates.

When Vittoria stepped up to the podium, Lana's ears pricked up. She spoke eloquently about how much she had learned from Matteo and how greatly he was missed by his employees. When Vittoria wiped away a tear, Lana had to resist standing and applauding her performance. She knew firsthand that Matteo was not as friendly or kind as the acting CEO was making him out to be.

An older, well-dressed man took to the podium next and began by thanking the crowd for honoring his friend by attending. "Matteo and I went to university together, and I have him to thank for my first job and career in the cruise ship industry. He even hired my daughter when her job prospects were quite poor—for that I am eternally grateful. He was a good man and one I was proud to call my friend."

When the man began weeping openly, Bianca went up and comforted him. Lana was confused as to why she did so, until she heard Bianca call the man "papa."

No wonder she wasn't fired earlier, Lana thought. Her father was a dear friend of Matteo. Bianca must have messed up repeatedly and royally if he saw no other option but to let her go. Come to think of it, Lana realized, Vittoria had also made a few snide remarks about how incompetent Bianca was, during the masquerade ball.

Bianca's father was the last to speak. After Bianca helped her father back to his seat, the priest wrapped up the funeral service, and Matteo's casket was carried by six pallbearers to an adjoining hall.

The guests trailed slowly behind, most with their heads bowed in respect. The rather plain hall was not what Lana had envisioned, given the high expectations that "funeral of the year" had conjured up, but was soon joyous enough for a wake.

Tuxedoed waiters wove through the masses, offering drinks and appetizers. Through the crowd, Lana caught glimpses of Vittoria, George, and the Windsor crew, but noted that they were not clustered together. Lana looked again to the acting CEO as she pressed palms and offered reassurances that the company would continue on, to all she passed. The way Vittoria flitted from group to group reminded Lana of a butterfly searching for nectar.

A million ways of approaching Vittoria went through Lana's head. Should she confront her directly? Or beat around the bush and hope Vittoria slipped up? As much as she wanted to pull her aside and wring the truth out of her, this was not the place to do so. Besides, it would take a miracle to get her alone; Vittoria was far too busy making the rounds. Her hopes of interrogating her prime suspect dashed, Lana resigned herself to waiting until later, when hopefully fewer visitors would be present. Then she would maybe have a chance to corner her prey.

She mingled with the crowd, in search of a waiter carrying drinks. Close by, a group's conversation revolved around Matteo's killer and where the police were in their investigation.

"What a relief that they caught the creep that murdered him!"

"I know, Matteo's soul can rest easy, knowing his killer is in prison."

"At least he is a foreigner—it would have broken my heart if an Italian had killed him."

The woman standing in front of Lana chimed in, "I heard they are trying to reinstate the death penalty, especially for the American."

Lana's heart about stopped, when the woman's husband added, "No, you heard it wrong. They are going to send him back to America where he can receive the death penalty. Why would Italy want to dirty its hands with that evil foreign blood? Let the Americans clean up their own mess."

She had to pinch her arm, to keep herself from bursting into tears. It was all assumptions and gossip, but it still cut deep to hear them talk so casually about the man she loved.

She rushed away from the couple, needing to distance herself from their horrid conversation. When she stopped to catch her breath and regain her composure, Lana spotted Vittoria straight ahead. And, as if by some miracle, she was standing alone.

Lana charged towards her target, ready to get this interrogation over with so that she could leave this blasted funeral, just as the Fretwells crossed her path first.

"George and Chrissy!" Vittoria cried out before kissing them both on the cheeks. "I cannot thank you enough for your help. Thanks to that little stunt we pulled at the restaurant yesterday, I am now earning ten percent more than Matteo did."

George slapped her on the back. "That's great news! And I take it you are still planning on rewarding me for my help?"

"Generously. Shall we start with a drink?"

35

Upsetting Rhonda

When Vittoria and the Fretwells walked over to the bar, Lana wanted to run after them and confront the acting CEO, just to get it over with. But she knew this was neither the time nor place to do so.

Instead, Lana decided to cut her losses. *What was I thinking, coming here?* she scolded herself as a wave of hopelessness rolled over her. *I'm not an investigator or a cop. Alex's lawyer will have to solve this one.*

As she walked towards the door, Lana passed Carmen and Rhonda deep in conversation. Both were gesturing animatedly at Bianca, and for the first time since this trip began, Rhonda looked angry.

Wondering what could be troubling her client, she crossed over to them.

"Lana, did you see her earrings? I bet she got a better deal because she's a local."

Rhonda sounded so put out, Lana had to look to see which earrings she meant. Indeed, Bianca had on the yellow sapphire earrings that Rhonda had fallen in love with. "That salesman refused to lower his price for me, remember?" she grumbled. "I noticed she was wearing them when she went up to comfort her father at the funeral."

"Are you certain that it's the same pair?" Lana stared at the jewelry, certain her eyes were deceiving her.

"Of course I am! The vintage setting and unusual stones make it unique. I am willing to stake my reputation that they are the same pair we saw in that antiques store yesterday afternoon."

Lana shook her head. "But how could she afford them? She told us she was at that antique shop to sell off trinkets so she could buy a bus ticket home. And those earrings cost two thousand dollars! If you had to sell your possessions to pay for transportation, why would you then splurge on those?"

Her voice trailed off as another thought entered her brain. "Unless she wasn't selling trinkets, but something worth much more. Rhonda, didn't you say that the gondola was worth somewhere between twenty and thirty thousand?"

When Rhonda nodded, Carmen and Lana locked eyes.

"If she sold the gondola statue to that antiques dealer, she could afford the earrings," Carmen said, speaking Lana's thoughts aloud.

Lana laid a hand on Rhonda's arm. "Do you remember which shop you saw them in?"

"Of course," Rhonda said confidently. "It was the third shop we went into."

Lana pulled out her phone and checked her map, glad she hadn't already cleared the search history. "Got it. I need to call the police. Wait—I better call Alex's lawyer first."

36

Unmasking a Killer

"We have to keep Bianca occupied until the police show up," Lana whispered to Carmen and Rhonda after she had called Salvatore Romano and caught him up.

"I just hope that antiques dealer hasn't already sold the gondola or lies about Bianca bringing it in."

Carmen wagged a finger at Lana. "Assuming she did steal it."

"Right now, I'm ninety-nine percent certain that Bianca did, but we'll know for certain soon enough. Alex's lawyer told the police about the antique shop, and he is sending his private investigator over there, as well. I just don't understand why Matteo had to die." Lana looked over at his assistant and shook her head. Bianca had been right in front of her the whole time, and she had never considered the young woman a viable suspect.

"Maybe it was a robbery gone wrong, after all," Carmen whispered.

Lana nodded slowly. "Bianca had access to the safe, and Matteo was going to fire her the next day—at least, that's what he threatened to do at the party. If she was going to steal it, that was probably her last chance to do so."

"If he caught her up in his office with the gondola, I can imagine he would have called the police," Carmen mused.

Lana watched as Bianca helped her father into his jacket. The older man was apparently still too devastated by his friend's death to do much more than weep. "And Matteo was a good friend of her father, by the look and sound of it. I can imagine their relationship would have suffered, as well."

When she noticed that Bianca and her father were waving goodbye to an elderly couple, she grabbed Carmen's arm. "She's leaving—we have to stop her!"

"Ow! Let go already, Stallone." After Lana released her grip, Carmen rubbed at her skin and nodded at Bianca.

"Let's head her off at the door. She's got her father on her arm; we should be able to beat them to it. Ready, Rhonda?" The three rushed over, apologizing as they pushed the funeral guests out of the way. Carmen was the first to arrive, followed closely by Lana. Rhonda's bulky frame made it tougher for her to maneuver through the crowd, and she soon fell behind.

"Bianca, wait!" Lana cried out as they converged by the front door.

The young woman turned towards her voice. "Oh, hi, Lana. I'm glad you were able to make it. Matteo would have been happy that you came—right, Papa?"

Her father nodded and smiled gently.

"We wanted to offer you our condolences, sir," Lana said, in a louder voice. "We heard you say at the funeral that you and Matteo were old friends."

"He was a good man," Bianca's father asserted, causing his daughter to roll his eyes.

"I should get Papa back to his hotel. It's been an emotional day."

"My, what lovely earrings," Lana said, as casually as she could. If Bianca detected the urgency in her voice, she could flee. "Where did you get them?"

Bianca tittered and looked nervously at her father, before softly responding, "These old things? My grandmother gave them to me years ago."

"You must have a very generous grandmother. When we saw you at the antiques store, you were about to sell a few objects you had inherited from her," Lana said in a loud voice that Bianca's father was certain to hear.

"What is she referring to, Bianca? Neither of your grandmothers left you any antiques." He leaned back on his heels and studied his daughter.

Before she could answer, Rhonda burst through the crowd, her jaw grinding. She whipped her arm out, pointing at Bianca's earrings. "Your grandma didn't give those to you. I saw that exact same pair in a shop yesterday! That antiques dealer wanted two thousand for those, but I know they aren't worth that much. How much did you pay for them?"

Lana had not yet seen her guest so riled up. Rhonda was apparently only concerned with having been denied a deal and seemed to have forgotten that Bianca may be a killer.

"What Rhonda meant to say," Lana rushed to add, hoping Bianca wouldn't try to leave, "is that they are quite distinctive. What a lovely present."

"Did you get a better deal because you are a local?" Rhonda pushed.

Bianca looked down her nose at Lana's guest, as if she was a piece of toilet paper stuck on her heel. "If you will excuse me, I have to get Papa to his hotel."

When she gently pushed her elderly father forward, Carmen and Lana locked eyes. Her guest grabbed the door handle and held it shut while Lana took ahold of Bianca's arm.

"What is the meaning of this?" her father yelled, drawing several guests' attention. When someone tried to pry Lana's arm off of Bianca's, she screamed out. "You can't let her leave—Bianca killed Matteo Conti! The police are on their way!"

Her father turned on Bianca, his face a mask of shame and anger. "You killed my friend? My own daughter…" He slipped to the floor, as if his knees had turned to jelly.

"Papa—can you hear me?" Bianca screamed as she tried to keep him upright, to no avail.

A voice rose from the crowd. "I am a doctor, let me through!" A middle-aged man pushed his way towards Bianca before checking her father's pulse and breathing.

"He is unconscious, but stable. We should call an ambulance, just in case."

Bianca knelt by her father's side and took his hand, kissing it while talking to him softly. A group of guests formed a large circle around the unconscious man, making certain that Bianca could not slip away.

Past experience made Lana pull out her phone and turn on the audio recorder before kneeling down by Bianca's side. If she was about to confess, Lana wanted to ensure the police would hear it, as well. "Why did you kill

Matteo, Bianca?"

"I didn't mean to," she cried, her eyes never leaving her father's face. Although he was unconscious, Lana could see his chest moving up and down at a normal rate.

When the young woman began softly weeping, Lana pushed her again. "What happened?"

Bianca hung her head low. "I was about to leave the party, knowing Matteo was going to fire me in the morning. The last person he let go was not allowed to clean out her desk, and I had to sneak her family photos to her, later. So I went up to collect my personal things. But as I walked up those stairs, I got madder and madder with each step. I deserved a raise for putting up with his crap, not to be fired."

"What do you mean?" Lana asked.

"Matteo may have been my father's friend, but he was also a sexist brute and a bully! I hated working for him. He was always changing his mind and then blaming me for not keeping up. And he was so degrading, it was as if he got pleasure from hurting people with his words. So I decided to hurt him with my actions. He was obsessed with that stupid statue, and I knew that if I stole it, it would drive him crazy. That's when I decided to take it, as payback for his horrible behavior."

Lana regarded the young woman, trying to work up a bit of sympathy for her. But Matteo's horrible behavior didn't justify stealing an expensive statue. "Did he catch you stealing the gondola? Is that why you hit him?"

Bianca nodded slightly. "I had just taken the gondola out of the safe when Matteo burst into his office. I don't know what he was doing up there, but as soon as he saw the statue in my hand, he immediately began cursing me out and threatening to call the police—and my papa." A tear rolled down Bianca's cheek as she gazed at her father's face.

Lana nodded, knowing that must have been the clincher.

"I have had trouble keeping my jobs in the past, and after I got behind with my rent a few times, my credit rating was ruined and it was impossible to find a decent apartment. My father swore that if I messed this job up, he would not help me with housing or employment ever again."

"So what did you do?"

"I begged Matteo not to tell anyone. I told him I would put the boat back in his safe and leave Venice right then and there. He would never see me again, he would still have his boat, and my father wouldn't have to know what had happened. But no, Matteo couldn't let it go. He called me worthless and all sorts of other horrible names, and then he picked up the phone to call the police. So I hit him with the boat."

Bianca shivered, as if she was reliving that horrible moment.

"The marble base came down harder than I anticipated. When he fell into his chair, his head hit the desk. After that, he stopped moving. It almost looked like he had fallen asleep while working, but there was so much blood. I didn't mean to kill him, I just wanted him to put the phone down and let me leave."

"What did you do then?" Lana whispered.

"I just had to get away from all that blood. When I ran out of his office, I saw the cleaner entering the kitchen, but she had headphones on and didn't turn in my direction, so I figured she didn't notice me. But there were voices on the stairs and lights on in several offices, so I ducked into a broom closet. Only then did I realize that the gondola was still in my hand. That's when I noticed there was blood on the marble base and statue, so I used the sink to wash it off. A few minutes later, I heard the cleaner screaming and several people calling out to each other. There was a bag in the broom closet big enough to hold the gondola. Once it grew quiet, I ran downstairs. I think Vittoria saw me in the hallway, but I'm not certain. It's a blur."

"How did you get out of the building?"

"That was easy enough. I'm an assistant—no one really notices me. I walked right out the front door with the gondola in a plastic Sail Away Cruises shopping bag. It felt appropriate." Bianca's tears had dried, and her head was held high.

"So Vittoria and the Earth Warriors didn't have anything to do with Matteo's murder?" Lana leaned in closer, praying her phone's microphone picked up Bianca's answer.

"No, nothing was planned or premeditated. If Matteo hadn't threatened to fire me, I would have kept working for the monster. I had no choice."

"Of course you did," Lana snapped. "No one forced you to keep working for him. Talking it out with your father would have been preferable to stealing that statue or murdering Matteo, don't you think?"

Bianca bit her lip and looked away.

Rhonda stepped forward and jutted her chin towards Bianca's jewelry. "Did you have the gondola statue with you when we met outside the antiques shop? Is that how you could afford those earrings?"

Bianca nodded, but kept her gaze averted.

Lana shushed her client, hoping to keep the conversation focused on Matteo. She assumed it was the shock that was making Bianca talk so freely and she didn't want her to wake from her daze and clam up. "But why did you stay in Venice instead of leaving town?"

"I was going to leave town after the party, but after I got back to my apartment, I realized that I couldn't take the gondola with me on the train or plane. No one would believe that it was a worthless tourist item. Plus, I was worried it might look suspicious if I left the next day. From the news, it sounded like the police were not interested in the statue's theft, so I decided to sell it here in Venice before I left."

The doors to the hall burst open, and a line of uniformed officers rushed inside. Leading the pack was Detective Esposito. His somber expression lightened slightly after he confirmed that Lana and her group were unharmed. While paramedics checked Bianca's father before taking him away on a stretcher, the detective pulled their new suspect aside and began questioning her.

Luckily for Lana, the young lady was so distraught, she honestly answered all of the officer's questions, repeating what she had done and why.

The detective's lips formed a thin line as he jotted down everything Bianca had to say. Lana could imagine he was as saddened by the young woman's confession as she was. No matter how horrible a person was, no one deserved to be murdered.

After he snapped his notebook shut and Bianca was handcuffed and taken outside, Lana approached the lead officer. "Detective Esposito, what does this mean for Alex Wright?"

He studied her intently before his eyes began to twinkle. "Ah, yes, Miss Lana Hansen. You failed to mention that you are in a relationship with our suspect. Or should I say, former suspect. I will personally see to it that your boyfriend is released immediately."

Tears of joy flowed freely down her cheeks, and Carmen wrapped her arms around her.

"You did it, Lana!" Carmen hugged her tight. "I knew it would all work out."

"I sure hope so," she replied, knowing that this was not the only problem that needed resolving.

37

Poor Taste

"Did the antiques dealer identify Bianca? And why didn't he ask for proof of ownership if that gondola statue was so expensive?" Dotty's confusion was audible through the phone line.

Lana stared down at the sparkling aquamarine water flowing through the canal below her hotel room's balcony, wondering how best to explain to her boss what exactly had transpired in the past few hours.

"Bianca told him it was a family heirloom she'd inherited, but that she had no place for in her apartment. He usually required proof of ownership, but that gondola is so ostentatious he assumed she was speaking the truth. No jeweler in their right mind would intentionally create something so vulgar to sell in their shop."

"I suppose it's a good thing that Matteo had bad taste."

Dotty's remark made Lana chuckle, for the first time in days. Now that Bianca was in police custody, her boyfriend was free. She had accompanied the detective back to the police station and had been waiting by the door when Alex was released. Their embrace was long and passionate, but she knew they still had much to discuss. Before they got into it, Alex wanted to get cleaned up, and Lana needed to catch her boss up on all that had occurred.

"I am tickled pink that Alex is free. But have you two had a chance to talk yet?" Dotty's voice was laced with concern.

She looked up as the bathroom door opened and her boyfriend walked out, with only a towel around his waist.

"No, we have not. But Alex just stepped out of the shower, so I think we are about to. But hey, Dotty, before I let you go, are you certain I can have a week off?"

"I am. Tom can take your place, which will save me from having to fly another guide over at the last minute."

"Great, then I'll talk to you later. Big hug, Dotty."

"Back at ya, Lana!"

She hung up and walked straight into Alex's strong arms. After allowing herself a moment to snuggle against his chest, Lana knew it was time for their heart-to-heart.

"How does it feel to be free?" she murmured into his bare skin.

"Wonderful, because now I can do this." He kept his arms around her and kissed the top of her head. "While I was in jail, all I could think about was how I had hurt you. That's what I regret most. All I want to do is go back to how it was. What do you say we spend the next few days making things right?"

When he pulled her lips up towards him, Lana tensed up, knowing this was the moment of truth. "What do you say to Newcastle upon Tyne? I've always wanted to see the Tyne Bridge."

She had purposely not mentioned the news footage of him taking part in other protests. This was his chance to come clean and bare his soul. Until he did, Lana knew they wouldn't be able to simply go back to how it was. She squeezed her eyes shut, hoping he would make the right decision.

Alex shrugged. "I was thinking of somewhere more romantic, but if that's where you want to go, then Newcastle it is."

She pulled out of his embrace. "That's all? Do you have anything else you want to say about the bridge?"

Alex ran a hand through his wavy hair. "It's not much to look at. I guess it's prettier at night because of the way it's lit up. What do you want me to say?"

Lana's laugh was low and bitter. "How about that you recently hung an

Earth Warriors sign off of it? It was all over the news."

Alex went as pale as a sheet of paper.

"I want to trust you, but I cannot if you refuse to tell me the whole truth—not just the bits you think I want to hear."

"I told you, I was worried about upsetting you."

Lana threw her arms over her torso and eyed him critically. "That's been your line this whole week. I'm not made of porcelain—you don't have to handle me with gloves."

Alex shook his head. "What is happening to us?"

"I don't know. But too much has happened to just sweep it all under the carpet and start again. I feel like I don't even know who you are anymore."

"Lana, I'm the same man you fell in love with!" The panic in his voice was distressing.

"That might be so, but I need to get my head straight before we can discuss whether we continue to see each other or not."

Alex began to protest again, but one look at Lana's face made him change tactic. "Please don't shut me out just yet. Give me another chance! I do love you, Lana Hansen, so very much."

"That's good to know." She kissed his nose. "I'll keep it in mind."

His eyes welled up. "What are you going to do?"

She sighed and cast her eyes downward. "I need to get away from work and you for a few days. I can't think rationally right now, and I don't want to make any long-term decisions until I can. But I promise to get in touch once I've had a chance to sort this out in my mind."

Alex hung his head hung low. "Then I better get dressed and go. I'm going to fly back to Seattle where I'll be waiting for you to call."

He tried pulling her in for another kiss, but Lana pushed him gently away. "I have to get back to my guests."

"Of course. Take care of yourself, my love."

"I'll be in touch soon." She could see his heart breaking, but Lana knew she had to do this—for herself.

38

Destination Unknown

April 27—Day Nine of the Wanderlust Tour in Venice, Italy

The last day of their tour had flown by. Carmen and Rhonda took Lana under their wing and did all they could to help her keep her mind off of Alex. She knew she owed it to both of them not to make any rash decisions. And until she could get away and be on her own, she wouldn't be able to get her head straight.

An hour after their guests had left the hotel, Lana was standing in front of a ticket window inside of the Santa Lucia Train Station. When it was her turn, she approached the ticket seller and noted that his hands were already hovering over his keyboard. "Where to?"

"I'd like a ticket on the next train leaving." Lana knew she sounded despondent, but right then, she couldn't have cared less.

"Are you running from the law?" the man joked, though Lana could hear nervousness in his voice. Considering the murder and polices chases dominating the news this week, it was understandable.

"No, from a broken heart."

The man ticked his tongue softly against his teeth, then pushed a ticket into her hand. "It's on the house," he whispered and smiled in a grandfatherly way.

Somehow, his kindness only made Lana feel worse.

190

She picked up the ticket, profusely thanked the man for his generosity, and then slipped outside to call Willow.

Her best friend answered on the first ring. "Where are you, Lana?"

"In Venice, but I'm about to catch a train out of town. This Alex situation is really doing my head in. I feel so lost, Willow. Do you have a minute to talk?"

"Of course. I always have time for you, my friend."

THE END

Thanks for reading *Death by Gondola*!

Reviews really do help readers decide whether they want to take a chance on a new author. If you enjoyed this story, please consider posting a review on BookBub, on Goodreads, or with your favorite retailer. I appreciate it!
Jennifer S. Alderson

Follow the further adventures of Lana Hansen in *Death by Puffin: A Bachelorette Party Murder in Reykjavik.*

Iceland—land of fire, ice ... and murder?

After a nasty fight with her boyfriend, tour guide Lana Hansen takes a week off work to get her head straight. Fate brings her to Iceland and the Hotel Puffin where she hopes the magnificent natural surroundings will help heal her heart and point the way forward.

Instead of the rest and relaxation she wishes to find, Lana ends up neighbors with a group of rowdy Americans in town for a bachelorette party and wedding. Their joyous frivolity is a painful reminder of her own relationship problems, and Lana does her best to steer clear of the group.

Yet when someone in the wedding party dies under mysterious circumstances, she gets pulled into the investigation. Can Lana help unmask the killer before they strike again—or will this trip be her last?

Available as paperback, large print edition, and eBook in 2022.

Acknowledgments

I want to thank my wonderful family for helping me create the time and space to write during the many lockdowns and school closures.

My editor, Sadye Scott-Hainchek of The Fussy Librarian, continues to do an excellent job polishing this series, and I am grateful for her outstanding work and advice. The cover designer for this series, Elizabeth Mackey, constantly amazes me with her gorgeous and fun designs.

I hope this book and the others in my Travel Can Be Murder series help to sate your wanderlust during these trying times. Stay safe, dear readers.

About the Author

Jennifer S. Alderson was born in San Francisco, grew up in Seattle, and currently lives in Amsterdam. After traveling extensively around Asia, Oceania, and Central America, she lived in Darwin, Australia, before settling in the Netherlands.

Jennifer's love of travel, art, and culture inspires her award-winning Zelda Richardson Mystery series, her Travel Can Be Murder Cozy Mysteries, and her Carmen De Luca Art Sleuth Mysteries. Her background in journalism, multimedia development, and art history enriches her novels.

When not writing, she can be found perusing a museum, biking around Amsterdam, or enjoying a coffee along the canal while planning her next research trip.

Sign up for Jennifer's website [https://jennifersalderson.com/] to receive updates on future releases, as well as two FREE short stories: A Book To Die For (cozy mystery) and Holiday Gone Wrong (mystery thriller).

Books by Jennifer S. Alderson:

Carmen De Luca Art Sleuth Mysteries
Collecting Can Be Murder
A Statue To Die For
Forgeries and Fatalities
A Killer Inheritance

Travel Can Be Murder Cozy Mysteries

Death on the Danube: A New Year's Murder in Budapest
Death by Baguette: A Valentine's Day Murder in Paris
Death by Windmill: A Mother's Day Murder in Amsterdam
Death by Bagpipes: A Summer Murder in Edinburgh
Death by Fountain: A Christmas Murder in Rome
Death by Leprechaun: A Saint Patrick's Day Murder in Dublin
Death by Flamenco: An Easter Murder in Seville
Death by Gondola: A Springtime Murder in Venice
Death by Puffin: A Bachelorette Party Murder in Reykjavik

Zelda Richardson Art Mysteries
The Lover's Portrait: An Art Mystery
Rituals of the Dead: An Artifact Mystery
Marked for Revenge: An Art Heist Thriller
The Vermeer Deception: An Art Mystery

Standalone Travel Thriller
Down and Out in Kathmandu: A Backpacker Mystery

Death by Puffin: A Bachelorette Party Murder in Reykjavik

Book Nine of the Travel Can Be Murder Cozy Mystery series

Iceland—land of fire, ice … and murder? After a nasty fight with her boyfriend, tour guide Lana Hansen takes a week off work to get her head straight. Fate brings her to Iceland and the Hotel Puffin where she hopes the magnificent natural surroundings will help heal her heart and point the way forward.

Instead of the rest and relaxation she wishes to find, Lana ends up neighbors with a group of rowdy Americans in town for a bachelorette party and wedding. Their joyous frivolity is a painful reminder of her own relationship problems, and Lana does her best to steer clear of the group.

Yet when someone in the wedding party dies under mysterious circumstances, she gets pulled into the investigation. Can Lana help unmask the killer before they strike again—or will this trip be her last?

Excerpt from *Death by Puffin*
Chapter One: Storm Brewing

Sunday—Reykjavik, Iceland

Lana Hansen stared outside, taking in the storm brewing over Faxaflói Bay. Gale-force winds whipped rain and hail across her hotel's windows, temporarily blurring her view of Mount Esja, rising high above Reykjavik's skyline.

Despite the breathtakingly beautiful sight before her, Lana couldn't enjoy it. Right now, it felt as if the turbulent weather mirrored the storm raging in her heart and mind. Her job and relationship were both on the fritz, and after a week of soul-searching, she still couldn't see a way out of either predicament.

I really need to talk to Willow, Lana moaned internally, knowing it was not possible. Willow Jeffries was Lana's best friend and one of the most sensible people she had ever met. Whenever Lana had a problem, Willow managed to cut right to the heart of the matter and often offered her a perspective she had not yet considered. Yet as much as Lana wanted to call her, it was the middle of the night in Seattle; she couldn't risk waking up Willow's baby girl, Zoe. Knowing her best friend was effectively unavailable sank her into a deeper depression, so much so that she barely registered the knock on her hotel room door.

Only when the knocks increased in intensity and frequency did Lana snap out of her daze and rise to answer the door.

Did I order room service and forget about it? she wondered as a troubling thought struck. *Am I having temporary lapses in consciousness now, on top of everything else?*

"Lana Hansen, I know you are in there. Open up," her visitor insisted.

The person's voice caused her to sprint to the door and yank it open. When she saw the petite African American woman standing in her doorway, she blurted out, "What are you doing here?"

The woman's hands flew to her hips. "Is that any way to greet your best friend?"

"No, it most certainly is not." Lana pulled Willow in for a hug, careful not to tug on the plethora of tiny braids cascading down her back. "I seriously thought I was hallucinating. I was just wishing I could call you, and now you're standing in my doorway. I can't believe that you are here!"

"Me, either," Willow laughed. "Are you going to invite me into your room?"

"Of course, come on in." Lana stepped aside. To her delight, Willow had a large suitcase with her. "Gosh, how long are you planning on staying?"

Instead of answering, Willow let her bag fall to the floor as her hand flew to her nose. "What is that smell?"

She laid a hand on Lana's arm. "What happened here—were you robbed and they trashed the place? Or are you having a breakdown?"

Lana looked around the space with a critical eye. Dirty cups were stacked on top of the minibar, and used towels hung off of the backs of the chairs and furniture. But the *pièce de résistance* was Lana's bed. The sheets and pillows were twisted up into a tower-like mass and covered with a scattering of crumbs and candy bar wrappers.

"Tracey Emin could turn your bed into a work of art," Willow said, no hint of a joke in her voice.

Lana grimaced. She only knew about the contemporary artist's installations—her most famous featuring her own unkempt bed—because of Willow. Her best friend loved to visit Seattle's many museums and galleries far more than she did.

Still, Lana couldn't get past her friend's sudden arrival. "Seriously—what are you doing here? You have a beautiful baby girl at home who needs your care and attention far more than I do."

"And a wonderful partner who was willing and able to take a few days off work to care for her." Willow took Lana's hands and smiled. "Besides, Dotty promised to help out."

"I don't know how good she is with kids," Lana grumbled.

"Look, I am certain Zoe will be well-cared for, so stop worrying about her for me. You sounded so depressed the last few times we talked, I was really worried about you. And after Dotty caught me up to speed, even more so. I have seven whole days to spend with my bestie to try to help her—that means you—get out of this crazy slump. At least, if you don't mind a roommate."

Lana threw her arms around Willow as she choked back her tears. "Thank you so much for coming over. I really need a friend right now. I feel so lost, I just don't know what to do anymore."

"I figured as much, which is why I knew a long video chat wouldn't be enough to sort this out." She rubbed Lana's back and let her cry it out for a moment, before gently pulling out of their embrace.

"However, I cannot sleep in a room this dirty. We are going to have to let the hotel cleaners back inside, but we should probably tidy up a little bit first, so they don't throw you out."

Willow gazed around, apparently taking in the sorry state of Lana's room, before asking, "I know you told Dotty you needed time to get your head sorted, but this is not what I expected. Have you been holed up here since you arrived?"

"Pretty much. I didn't come here to see the sights."

Willow's deep sigh sent a wave of irritation over Lana. "What did you think I was doing—hiking a glacier or soaking in a hot spring? Alex broke my heart, and my boss thinks I'm a magnet for murderers. I haven't been having the best month. Can't I just lie here and wallow in self-pity for a few more days?"

When Willow's frown deepened, Lana plopped back down onto the couch and pulled a blanket over her head. *Maybe if I stay under here, she will leave me be.*

Willow's laugh was not friendly as she tore the blanket off. "Frankly, I hoped that was exactly what you were doing. You are in Iceland—I figured this was therapy by nature. Come on, it's time to rectify this situation."

Willow held out her hand.

Lana pushed further back into the couch's fluffy cushions and reflected on her friend's statement. "How are we going to do that?"

"I've booked us in at the Blue Lagoon. Our bus leaves in an hour."

Lana shook her head. "I'm not ready to mingle with tourists. Can't we use the hotel spa, instead?"

"No, we need to get you out of this room and back into the world. That might be the only way for you to get over this wallowing depression, because this…" Willow glanced again around the dirty space. "…is not normal. Besides, I bet if you allow your mind to focus on other things, it will be easier for you to see your problems from a distance. And if we are lucky, we can figure out the solution to both of them, together."

"You aren't going to take no for an answer, are you?"

Willow shook her head.

"Then I have no choice but to go with you. Let me find my coat."

Willow grimaced as she sniffed in her friend's direction. "Even though we are going to a pool, I still think you should shower first and change into something clean. You don't smell fresh."

Lana looked down at her stained and crumpled clothes. When had she changed last? Or showered?

Willow pulled open the chest of drawers. "It's empty. Where are your clothes?"

Lana pointed to her suitcase, open on the floor next to her bed.

"You haven't even unpacked yet?" her friend cried. "You truly are a mess."

She pulled a T-shirt and jeans out of the suitcase, then tossed them to Lana as she walked towards the bathroom. "These look relatively clean."

Lana snatched them out of the air and pulled the T-shirt up to her nose, using it to cover her reddening cheeks. "Thanks. I'll be back in a minute."

* * *

If you are enjoying the story, why not pick it up now and keep reading? Available as paperback, large print edition, eBook, and in Kindle Unlimited.

The Lover's Portrait: An Art Mystery

Book One in the Zelda Richardson Art Mystery Series

"*The Lover's Portrait* is a well-written mystery with engaging characters and a lot of heart. The perfect novel for those who love art and mysteries!" – Reader's Favorite, 5 star medal

"Well worth reading for what the main character discovers—not just about the portrait mentioned in the title, but also the sobering dangers of Amsterdam during World War II."
– IndieReader

A portrait holds the key to recovering a cache of looted artwork, secreted away during World War II, in this captivating historical art thriller set in the 1940s and present-day Amsterdam.

When a Dutch art dealer hides the stock from his gallery—rather than turn it over to his Nazi blackmailer—he pays with his life, leaving a treasure trove of modern masterpieces buried somewhere in Amsterdam, presumably lost forever. That is, until American art history student Zelda Richardson sticks her nose in.

After studying for a year in the Netherlands, Zelda scores an internship at the prestigious Amsterdam Historical Museum, where she works on an exhibition of paintings and sculptures once stolen by the Nazis, lying unclaimed in Dutch museum depots almost seventy years later. When two women claim the same painting, the portrait of a young girl entitled *Irises*, Zelda is tasked with investigating the painting's history and soon finds evidence that one of the two women must be lying about her past. Before she can figure out which one it is and why, Zelda learns about the Dutch art dealer's concealed collection. And that *Irises* is the key to finding it all.

Her discoveries make her a target of someone willing to steal—and even kill—to find the missing paintings. As the list of suspects grows, Zelda realizes she has to track down the lost collection and unmask a killer if she wants to survive.

Excerpt from *The Lover's Portrait*
Chapter 1: Two More Crates

June 26, 1942

Just two more crates, then our work is finally done, Arjan reminded himself as he bent down to grasp the thick twine handles, his back muscles already yelping in protest. Drops of sweat were burning his eyes, blurring his vision. "You can do this," he said softly, heaving the heavy oak box upwards with an audible grunt.

Philip nodded once, then did the same. Together they lugged their loads across the moonlit room, down the metal stairs, and into the cool subterranean space below. After hoisting the last two crates onto a stack close to the ladder, Arjan smiled in satisfaction, slapping Philip on the back as he regarded their work. One hundred and fifty-two crates holding his most treasured objects, and those of so many of his friends, were finally safe. Relief briefly overcame the panic and dread he'd been feeling for longer than he could remember. Preparing the space and artwork had taken more time than he'd hoped it would, but they'd done it. Now he could leave Amsterdam knowing he'd stayed true to his word. Arjan glanced over at Philip, glad he'd trusted him. He stretched out a hand towards the older man. "They fit perfectly."

Philip answered with a hasty handshake and a tight smile before nodding towards the ladder. "Shall we?"

He is right, Arjan thought, *there is still so much to do.* They climbed back up into the small shed and closed the heavy metal lid, careful to cushion its fall. They didn't want to give the neighbors an excuse to call the Gestapo. Not when they were so close to being finished.

Philip picked up a shovel and scooped sand onto the floor, letting Arjan rake it out evenly before adding more. When the sand was an inch deep, they shifted the first layer of heavy cement tiles into place, careful to fit them snug up against each other.

As they heaved and pushed, Arjan allowed himself to think about the future for the first time in weeks. Hiding the artwork was only the first step; he still had a long way to go before he could stop looking over his shoulder. First, back to his place to collect their suitcases. Then, a short walk to Central Station where second-class train tickets to Venlo were waiting. Finally, a taxi ride to the Belgian border where his contact would provide him with falsified travel documents and a chauffeur-driven Mercedes-Benz. The five Rembrandt etchings in his suitcase would guarantee safe passage to Switzerland. From Geneva he should be able to make his way through the demilitarized zone to Lyon, then down to Marseilles. All he had to do was keep a few steps ahead of Oswald Drechsler.

Just thinking about the hawk-nosed Nazi made him work faster. So far he'd been able to clear out his house and storage spaces without Drechsler noticing. Their last load, the canvases stowed in his gallery, was the riskiest, but he'd had no choice. His friends trusted him—no, counted on him—to keep their treasures safe. He couldn't let them down now. Not after all he'd done wrong.

* * *

Pick up your copy now at your favorite retailer and keep reading! Available as paperback, audiobook, and eBook.

Made in the USA
Monee, IL
26 December 2023

50562541R00118